# A LEAD PILL

## A COLLECTION OF STORIES
## FROM A HARD PLACE
# BY R A JACOBSON

deadcatstudio

# R A JACOBSON

A Lead Pill
© 2021, R A Jacobson
Published by Deadcat Studio
illustrations by Rick Jacobson

rajacobson@deadcatstud.io

Tune in every Thursday to the "Stories from a Hard Place" podcast wherever you listen to your podcasts, or at Deadcatstud.io

While there, please join the mailing list. You can also check out the merchandise. Whether it's a t-shirt, a mug or a phone case, we got you covered.

If you are enjoying the world that Jacob and the other characters live in, HARD PLACE, the novel, will be released October 2021.
Sign up to be notified of the release date as well as that of the graphic novel currently in the works.

Join our mailing list at Deadcatstud.io

Book and Cover design by Deadcat Studio
text set in Century Old Style
ISBN: 978-1-990182-02-0

First Edition: March 2021

10 9 8 7 6 5 4 3 2 **1**

# CONTENTS

CHAPTER 1   Service Up               1

CHAPTER 2   Tired of Living         21

CHAPTER 3   Passing it Forward      31

CHAPTER 4   Haymaker                53

CHAPTER 5   The Refusal             69

CHAPTER 6   The Touch              111

CHAPTER 7   Adding it Up           169

He made a mistake, and now he's paying for it.

# CHAPTER 1

## SERVICE UP

Without looking at his watch, he knew it was time to get ready for the first customers in the diner. Donald walked out of his house, locked up and walked to the front of the restaurant.

To the east, the sky was promising a sunrise he would not see.

He paused and glanced at the building; it was tired. Although its heyday was long gone, Donald had spent every day of his life working there. He had no idea what he would do if he didn't wake up early to open. He told himself he liked the routine, that he liked cooking for people. He didn't think about how few customers he had, nor that they were dwindling monthly. Some were just dying off, some were moving out of the community, and some just got bored with coming.

The menu was exactly as it had been since his dad had written it out on a scrap of paper so many years ago. Donald remembered the joy in his father's face as he decided what his diner would serve. His parents, sitting at their tiny kitchen table,

1

had laughed as they made increasingly ridiculous suggestions about what they could serve. Donald had thought some ideas were pretty good, and had said so. They had laughed even harder.

He had been hurt by their laughter. His mom hugged him, and his dad added the cheesy macaroni and hotdogs with a splash of ketchup to the menu just for him. Although still on the menu, Donald couldn't recall the last time anyone had ordered it.

He unlocked the door and flipped on the lights. It wasn't a big diner, only four booths against the window, eight stools at the counter, and a single table in the corner.

Years ago, when his dad had gotten sick, Donald had taken over the diner and had put a reserved sign on that single table. He had never removed it. He had never allowed anyone to sit at the table. It was set for two.

He looked at the table in the far corner of the room. After a minute, his head fell, and he turned and went into the kitchen. As the flattop warmed up, he chopped onions, red and green peppers.

An hour later, the first customer walked in. It was Gordon, a trucker Donald had known for most of his life. Gordon walked past Donald, nodded absently, and sat down in the last booth. Donald watched Gordon for a second. Gordon had always sat at the counter and told jokes till his meal came. No jokes, no conversation, not even a smile. Something was up.

Donald glanced up at the clock on the wall. It was nearly 7:30. Where was Sheri Ann? He checked his wristwatch. She was late. He looked out the window. Across the parking lot he could see her hunched against the cold half-running, half-walking towards the diner. Seconds later, she burst through the door pink-faced, fogged-up glasses, and breathing hard.

"Morning. Sorry I'm late. My car wouldn't start," she said as she rushed past him, hung up her coat and put on her apron.

"It's fucking freezing!" She called from the back room, "Isn't it supposed to be warm at least for a month more?"

Donald smiled and went back to the kitchen. He glanced at Gordon. Gordon was staring at his hands.

Sheri Ann came out of the back, tying on her apron.

"Sorry," she smiled at Donald, "was it busy?" She laughed at her joke.

Donald smiled. "Just Gordon."

"K," she said and grabbed a glass of water and a cutlery roll-up.

Donald heard her ask Gordon how he was but couldn't hear his answer. Sheri Ann came back, started pouring coffee, "He's not himself," she frowned and went to deliver the mug. Donald looked through the pass-through at Gordon.

"The usual," she said. Which meant bacon, eggs and toast.

Donald got going on the order, his mind on Gordon. He had been one of his father's friends and was the very first customer served. He had been coming for over forty years, once or twice a month. He never changed, never got any older, just walked in with a big friendly smile. Donald had asked his dad about that.

"Gordon has made a deal," his father had said, "He made a mistake, and now he's paying for it."

Donald hadn't understood at the time, but he did now. Gordon had sold his soul to The Judge. He wasn't sure for what but as Donald's dad grew older, got sick and died, Gordon stayed the same. His face never sagged, his spine never curved, and his hair never lost its colour.

He flipped Gordon's eggs just as the toast popped. He

3

plated the breakfast and set it on the pass-through where Sheri Ann was waiting. She picked it up and walked to Gordon's booth.

Gordon didn't look up. He just stared into his coffee cup. Sheri Ann waited a minute, then left. She looked at Donald and shrugged.

Donald felt like he should do something, maybe ask Gordon if he was alright. They had never had a real conversation, Donald realized. Every word that had passed between them had been jokes and pleasantries, except one time when he was sixteen.

Gordon had come out the back of the diner to have a smoke and found Donald sitting on a milk crate crying. Gordon had apologized and turned to go back in, then he stopped and asked, "Why so glum chum?"

Donald looked up, surprised.

"Nothing," he said, quickly wiping the tears away.

"Don't look like nuthin'," Gordon said. "Lemme guess. It's about a girl."

Donald looked up sharply.

"How'd I know? At your age, it always is." Gordon said. "Look, kid, this is just how it goes. The first one cuts deep. It leaves a scar, but in a week or a month, you will be on to someone new."

Donald looked at Gordon with fire in his eyes. His lips were tight.

"Right. She's the only one you will ever love. She's the ONE. Mark my word, you be over her in a week," Gordon smiled with understanding in his eyes, shook his head, and went back inside.

From the kitchen, Donald watched Gordon staring at his coffee, lost in whatever world he was focused on. Gordon had been wrong, was wrong. Donald hadn't gotten over her. Not in a week, not in a month, not ever.

He glanced at the reserved table, his monument, his shrine to her. It was there Donald had had his one and only date with her. He hadn't known how to date, how to act, where to take her, so he brought her here, the diner.

He had been sitting in the hallway at school when he had noticed her. She had walked by with several of her friends. They were all laughing and making jokes while she was quiet, smiling, playing with her hair. He had seen her later in the library reading. He couldn't see what she was reading, but she sat straight through third class, just reading and playing with her hair. She wound it around her left finger tight then let the curl unwind. Sometimes she tied a knot in it, then let it unravel. It took two weeks for him to find a moment when she was alone, and the courage to walk up to her, and even then, he nearly bailed, but she caught his eye, and he couldn't think of anything to say except his rehearsed question. She rocked on one hip looking at him, her left finger twirling her hair, then she smiled and said, "Sure."

He had borrowed his mom's station wagon. It was a long boat of a car, off-white with fake wood grain panels, and it smelt of cabbage and dog. He was so nervous as he stood out in front of her house for several long minutes building up the courage to ring the bell. When he did, he stood still, and willed himself not to run.

Her mom answered the door, smiling. She watched patiently as he stammered and finally asked, "Is Mary Lou home?"

Her mom smiled and said, "Yes, she'll be right out."
And she was. She stepped out of the house in jeans and a t-shirt.

Her long hair loose and a smile on her lips, "Hi, Don. Where are we going?"

Donald stuttered, opened the door for her, and managed to say, "We're going to the diner for supper, then I thought we'd go to the drive-in."

She looked at him and smiled, "The man with a plan. OK."

As they drove to the diner, Donald was keenly aware of the distance between them. The broad bench seat had room for four people to sit comfortably on it. Mary Lou sat close to her door, miles away from him.

He stopped at the diner, jumped out and hustled around the massive car to open her door. She was already out and standing waiting for him.

"This is your dad's diner, isn't it?" she asked.

"Umm, ya," he said.

As he opened the door to the diner, a thought crossed his mind. This might not have been such a great idea.

Inside, his dad sat them at the only table he had. It had a reserved sign on it.

"What can I get you two to drink?" Donald's dad asked as he handed them the large menus. Donald looked to Mary Lou.

"I would love a vanilla milkshake," she said as she took the menu.

"Same," Donald said. He winced as his dad winked at him. Yup, bad idea.

Mary Lou saw the wink and grinned. Donald tried not to notice. They sat in silence for a bit.

"What's showing at the drive-in?" Mary Lou asked.

"Um, I'm not sure," he said, realizing he should have found out. "Just a sec," and he stood and went to the front door of the diner where there was a community corkboard. It took him a minute to find the drive-in schedule. He found it buried under a handwritten paper selling a used grain truck.

It was a red sheet of paper with a calendar printed on it in black. He scanned the dates, and his heart sank. The big letters spelled out 'Retro Saturday Creature Feature.' Not great date movies. He would love them, but he suspected Mary Lou wouldn't.

Girls didn't like horror movies. At least that's what his mom had said.

He went back to the table, feeling disappointed. He should have checked. Now, what are they going to do? His dad had told him to have a plan. He said women liked it when a man takes charge. So acting on his dad's dating advice, he had thought about it and made a plan. He thought he had it figured out, but he was wrong.

"It's a double creature feature. They're having a retro night," he said as he sat, braced for her disappointment.

"Really?" she said. "What are the movies?" She seemed excited.

He paused. "Um, Creature from the Black Lagoon and Revenge of the Creature."

"Cool! In 3-D?" She leaned forward.

"I don't think so," he said, unsure.

"Too bad, but still cool!" she grinned at him.

"So, you like horror movies?" he asked.

"Hell yes. They're fantastic! Especially the old Hammer movies."

"Hammer movies?"

"Ya! Wait, you don't know about Hammer?" she asked.

He shook his head.

"The Curse of Frankenstein, Dracula, The Mummy, Bride of Frankenstein, The Invisible Man?"

Donald shrugged. He had heard the titles and maybe seen parts of them on TV late at night but didn't know them. Mary Lou was really into this. Inside, he congratulated himself on a good plan.

"You haven't seen them?" she asked.

He shook his head.

"These are classics!" She sat back. "Hammer put out some of the best horror flicks ever. Hammer and, of course, Roger Corman."

He looked at her blankly.

"House of Usher?" she asked.

Again, he shook his head.

"You've never seen House of Usher?" she crossed her arms and shook her head, "You poor boy, you have been deprived."

She leaned forward, "Well…"

And she launched into a long discussion about horror films. It was a very one-sided conversation.

Donald listened, mesmerized.

She paused to order a burger and fries when Donald's dad returned, then kept on going. Even when the food arrived, she continued. She paused again to take a bite, then talked with her mouth half full.

Donald ate and listened, amazed.

She only slowed when they were finishing their meal, and she paused to take a sip of her milkshake. She looked at him over her glass as she sucked on the last drops of her shake.

He looked at her, at her eyes as she regarded him. They were open and bright, full of intelligence and curiosity.

He wasn't sure what he felt. It was a bit like when he

fainted at the fair a couple of years ago. His heart sped up, he started to sweat, and the edges of his sight darkened. He looked at her through a tunnel. She filled his mind. Amid the loud sucking sounds of her finishing her shake, a thought entered his mind. This is what love feels like. A sort of panic raced over him.

She beamed at him, and he grinned back.

The next four hours blended into the most fantastic time. He came out of his shyness. He talked about things he loved, about comics, books and drawing. He told her things he had never told anyone. She laughed and talked about movies mostly, but halfway through 'The Revenge,' she started talking about music and singing.

She got quiet. He strained to hear. She said she wanted to be a singer. She said she wanted more than anything to sing on stage. Then even quieter, she said, "And I'll go see the Judge if that's what it takes." She twirled her hair, and looked sideways at him.

At first, he wasn't sure if he had heard her. He leaned forward, tipping his head slightly. Then he realized he understood what she had said, he just couldn't believe it. He sat back, unsure of what to say. He was shocked. Everything he had heard about the Judge was bad.

She looked at him, reading his reaction. She looked away. They sat, not talking for the rest of the movie.

He started the car and slowly lined up to leave the drive-in. They sat still, their headlights on the vehicle ahead for several minutes.

"That was great!" She looked at him, "Thank you for taking me."

He smiled, sensing something had changed.

"It was cool. You know a lot about these movies," he said.

They finally got out of the drive-in and onto the highway. They talked about school a bit, and about teachers they liked. Halfway to Mary Lou's home, the conversation died utterly. They sat in silence. They pulled up to the front of her home and stopped.

Mary Lou turned, "Thank you, Don. I had a wonderful time." With a smile, she opened her door and slid out.

"See you at school," she said, then she closed the door and walked to her house. She waved as she went inside.

Donald stared after her for a minute.

Was that a good date or a bad one?

He drove home, running over the date in his mind again and again. Parts of it were great; in fact, most of it was perfect. It was just the last bit.

Donald saw Mary Lou at school, but he never got a chance to talk with her. He started to obsess over the date. Every time he reassessed the date downward until he knew it had been a disaster.

He thought about her constantly. He waited in the hallways at school that he knew she walked down. It became apparent she was avoiding him. Then he saw her getting into a beat-down Chevy truck with a guy. He watched as she slid across the bench seat to sit right beside him. He watched them kiss and felt pain like he had never known before. It took his breath as if he had been punched in the gut.

He ran home, trying not to cry, and failing.

He stayed home for a couple of days. When he went back, he avoided anywhere she might be. He didn't see her, not that day nor the next. It was Friday when he saw her. She was walking outside, holding hands with a tall boy. Donald thought his name was Jacob.

A week later, he heard the worst news he could have ever heard.

Mary Lou was killed, run over by her boyfriend. It was all over the news, on tv, in the newspaper, and everyone was talking about it at school. There was a tremendous amount of conversation about whether or not Jacob had run her over on purpose. Some thought Jacob was a no-good yahoo and probably was drunk. Others thought it had been just a terrible accident. Even his folks talked about it at the dinner table. Donald tried not to listen, but it was nearly impossible not to hear when it was all around him.

There was an investigation. It went on for weeks. Eventually, Jacob was found innocent, the cause declared to be a mechanical malfunction in the brand-new truck Jacob had been driving. Many people still thought Jacob was guilty, but it didn't really matter to Donald. Every minute of every day, he thought about Mary Lou. She never faded from his heart. And in some 40 years, no one had come along to replace her.

Donald pulled his mind from the past and looked over to Gordon. Even though Gordon was probably in his late 70s, he looked half Donald's age.

"Gordon, what's up?" he asked.

After a minute, Gordon looked up, his eyes coming from far away. "Hey, Donald. Oh, jus' got a problem I'm werkin' through."

"Well, is there anything I kin help with?" Donald asked.

Gordon looked at him for a long time, considering, "No. I suppose you know that ah made a deal sometime back."

Donald slid into the booth opposite Gordon. "Ya, dad told me, I guess right after you did it. He didn't seem happy about it."

"No. It was one of the worst fights we had. He wouldn't talk to me for quite a spell."

"He never talked to me about it after that one time, and he never did tell me what you sold for," Donald said. Sheri Ann stood beside them, a hand on her hip.

"You want a coffee?" she asked Donald.

"Ya, thanks," Donald looked up as Sheri Ann left to get the coffee.

"It's not important," Gordon said, "like all deals, it was stupid, very stupid."

Donald had known for a long time what he would sell his soul for, known since he was sixteen and broken hearted but knowing and doing he found out were very different things.

Sheri Ann returned with two cups of coffee and slid into the booth beside Donald.

Donald took the coffee, "Thanks."

Gordon looked at Sheri Ann as she sipped on her coffee, shrugged, and continued, "Well, I may have found a way out. I think just maybe I have a secret that can release me from my deal."

Donald and Sheri Ann looked at Gordon, then to each other.

"That's not possible." Sheri Ann said, "My brother did a deal with the Judge. A little over six years later, he was dead. Never found out what he sold for. Just fucking stupid if you ask me."

"Ya, I've never heard of anyone getting out of their deal, not ever," Donald said.

"Well, ya yer right, but I know something, something that will make a difference," Gordon said.

"What is it?" Sheri Ann asked.

"I can't tell you. Wouldn't make any sense to you, anyway. Neither of you being marked."

"Marked?"

"That's what it's called when you make a deal. You are marked. In fact, there is a mark, a soot smudge on the forehead of everyone that has made a deal," Gordon said.

"I've never seen that," Sheri Ann said, Donald nodding beside her.

"Well, ah course not. Ya gotta be marked ta see it." Gordon frowned, "Anyway, I think I got a chance, but I gotta do something that's a bit dangerous, and I'm not sure bout it." Donald looked at Gordon.

"What are you contemplating doin'?" he asked.

"I'm going to kill the Judge," Gordon said.

"Kill the Judge? You can't kill the Judge. He's the devil. How in hell kin you kill the devil?" Donald asked.

"I said, TRY to kill the Judge. I just want to git his attention, then I kin force him to let me go," Gordon replied.

"I still don't get it," Sheri Ann said.

Gordon smiled as if a great weight lifted.

"This is gonna werk!" he said. "Thanks. I weren't sure, but jus' saying it out loud has made up my mind."

"What? I'm confused," Donald said, "What's goin' on?"

"I'm going to the crossroads tonight to have another meetin' with the Judge," Gordon took a sip of coffee.

"I thought once you went, the Judge would never show again for you. Didn't Jacob just about camp out there for months after Mary Lou died?" Sheri Ann asked.

"Yup, but I know that there's a young fellow meeting with

him tonight. Know it fer sure. I'm just gonna bust in," Gordon said and grinned and dug into his breakfast.

Sheri Ann looked at Gordon, then at Donald and shrugged, "You done, hun?" she asked Donald.

"Huh?" he said, "Ya, thanks."

Sheri Ann stood, picked up the cups and left.

Donald watched Gordon eat.

"So, you've made up yer mind?"

Gordon nodded, his mouth full of egg and toast. He paused chewing and grinned.

"Ok, then. Let me know how it goes," Donald said as he pulled himself from the booth. He stood for a second watching Gordon, then turned and went back to the kitchen.

Several minutes later, he heard Gordon telling a joke to Sheri Ann as he paid for his breakfast. Gordon laughed, and Donald heard the bell above the door ring as Gordon left.

Donald realized that if things went well tonight, he probably would never see Gordon again. He wished he had stayed and talked with him longer. He never said goodbye. A sadness slipped over him.

"Well, he was in better spirits," Sheri Ann said as she walked into the kitchen.

"Ya. I'm not sure what he's planning," he said.

"Oh, he'll tell us next time he's in, in great detail," she said and laughed.

"Maybe not. If it works like he thinks, he may never come back. Remember, he's an old man now, even if he doesn't look it."

"Shit, I never thought of that! I'm going to miss him."

"Yup, me too."

They were quiet for a minute, then the bell rang, and Sheri Ann left to seat the new customers.

The rest of the day went by as days do. Customers came and went. Donald shifted from eggs to burgers then at about 8:30 he started cleaning up, scraping down the flat top.

By nine, Sheri Ann had her coat on. Donald let her out. He flipped the lights off and locked up.

"See you tomorrow," she said over her shoulder.

"See you tomorrow," he said and walked around the diner to the back of the building where he lived. It was cold, not see your breath cold, but cold enough.

He unlocked his small home. It had changed little since it was his parents'. It had settled. The sagging couch, half-covered with an old blanket, sat against one wall. The chairs were all threadbare. Time had worn everything down. Like the diner, its best days were long past. With a sigh, he sat heavily in his chair. He sank in as it moulded to his familiar body. He turned on the tv. Nothing was on, there never was, but it killed time. He flipped the channels aimlessly, then turned the tv off.

Midnight was still a couple of hours away. He thought about Gordon. Donald wished he had asked more questions, found out more about what Gordon knew.

He pushed himself from the chair, his decision made. He grabbed his truck keys from the plate that had been by the door since before he was born, and where his dad's keys had been for so many years before his own had replaced them.

His truck squawked as he climbed in. He backed up, the transmission growling, and turned the headlights on as he pulled out onto the highway.

He knew where he was going. What he had told no one, even after forty years, is that he knew exactly where the crossroads were.

In twenty minutes, he pulled off 89, half a mile from the crossroads, and turned off the truck.

15

He looked up at the sky. It was dark, with no moon but thousands of stars. He walked across the field until he could see the crossroads. He sat down to wait. After a few minutes, he realized it wasn't as dark as he'd first thought. As he looked around, he could see the yard lights of several farms, some near, many farther away. To the east, he could see a soft glow from the city. He became aware of the small sounds of the night. Small creatures going about their nightly business. The grass rustled off to his left, an owl called, and further off, a coyote yipped.

He sat for a while, enjoying the air when he heard a rattling. In the distance, a truck was coming. Donald perked up as the truck drove into sight. He recognized it. It belonged to an old farmer named Allen. He and his wife came to the diner for lunch every once in a while. The truck rattled along. It slowed as it approached the crossroads. It made a turn, then stopped. Its headlights pointed almost directly at Donald. Even though he was far enough away he could not be seen, he crouched lower.

The headlights were weak, but they turned the black around Donald solid. He closed his eyes, hoping to get his night vision back. When he opened his eyes, the truck was pulling away from a lone figure, barely visible, standing at the crossroads.

The truck rattled away, and the night returned to the quiet. Donald watched the figure as he set down a guitar case and looked around.

The roar of a V8 engine split the quiet. Bright headlights came on, lighting the figure from the waist down and the road beyond. The figure spun, surprised by the sudden appearance of the car.

As Donald watched, a tall man in a suit stepped out. Donald knew this man. It was the Judge.

The two figures stood in the car's headlights, talking. Donald could hear their voices, but not what was being said. The figure handed the guitar case to the Judge, then pulled a gun on him. Donald strained to see what would happen next when he heard from his right the sound of a semi. Donald looked but saw nothing there. Then just as the semi reached the two figures standing on the road, the lights flared on, and the semi-truck crashed into them.

With a smashing, roaring sound that carried across the fields, the truck crashed violently into the car. From his position, Donald could not see what had happened to the two men. The truck, he realized, was Gordon's rig. It careened into the ditch and rolled over.

It was quiet again except for the tinkle of broken glass and the tick of hot metal.

The Judge came walking back onto the road, straightening his tie. Behind him, the car re-formed with a shimmer like heat over the blacktop. Donald saw the other man stand up and walk toward the ditch where Gordon had stepped from the wreckage of his rig. Gordon staggered, then fell. The man knelt beside him.

Donald didn't want to see any more. He was sure he had seen his friend die. He had known him for as long as he was alive. Gordon was more than just a friend. He had been family.

Donald, crouching in the tall grass, crept back to his truck and, as quietly as he could, headed back the way he had come. He didn't turn the lights on till he was sure he was far enough down the road.

He wasn't sure what it all meant. With Gordon dead, did that mean he was now in hell, or was he free from the Judge?

Did Gordon actually get what he wanted? He didn't think he would ever know.

The next morning, Donald woke up late and had to rush to get the diner open on time. Sheri Ann was late again, but only by a few minutes, and it really didn't matter, there were no customers.

It was nearing 10. One booth had a couple having breakfast. A trucker had stopped for coffee and was sitting at the bar when a very new-looking rig pulled in. Its air brakes hissed, and Gordon jumped down with a grin on his face. He marched across the parking lot and stepped into the diner.

"Morning," he called with a big grin.

"Gordon! I didn't expect to see you again," Donald said.

Gordon sat down at the counter grinning, "Whachu talkin' bout?"

"All that shit you were spoutin' bout yesday?"

Gordon's grin shrivelled slightly, "Oh, that. That weren't nothin'."

Donald looked at him. Gordon looked back, his smile split his face, "Hey, did you see my new rig?"

Donald glanced out to the parking lot at the shiny cab-over semi-trailer.

"Ya. Ya, I saw. Looks sharp."

"She's a beaut," Gordon said, still grinning.

Donald looked at Gordon for a second, "Same Ol'?"

"Yup! The usual." Gordon said with a big grin.

Donald smiled back, then returned to the kitchen and got to work on Gordon's food. He didn't see when Gordon left. His day continued and ended as so many had before. A constant routine that his father had followed and that he too followed his entire life.

At the end of his day, he said goodnight to Sheri Ann, and locked up. He stood and looked out into the night.

He walked around back to his house. A truck roared by on the highway as he opened the door. He stood in the doorway of the house that had been his parents'. Donald looked around the small room. He noticed the sagging furniture, the single table, the tiny kitchen that his mom had spent time in and wondered, where was he in this house? In all the years he had been here, he had not changed one thing. It was his parents' house still.

He sat in his father's chair and thought of Gordon. He would never really know what happened after he left the crossroads. It was obvious Gordon would continue to serve the Judge. Donald thought of his own life. A life lived in service. He served every day of his life to a memory of the One. He had flipped eggs, burgers and kept a shrine to that memory of the One. He watched the world through the windows of his diner.

He smiled as he crawled into bed with his wife.

# CHAPTER 2

## TIRED OF LIVING

What is the cost of breathing? What is the price of a breath? How much would you pay to live longer? Even one more breath. What is that worth? How can it be measured? How can it be calculated?

He sat on his porch, coffee in hand, and watched the morning. He was up early today, earlier than he had been in weeks. It was just after 7. His wife was still upstairs in bed. There was time. No need to disturb her yet.

For most of his life, his days had started at six AM. The alarm clock was set and was never changed. Even on the weekends, he maintained his routine.

Now, in retirement, his routine had slipped. He hated it. He still woke at six, but with nothing to do. With no one waiting for him, he would roll over and sleep a bit more. Sometimes that was 15 minutes. More often, it was an hour or more. His wife had continued her routine. Up at seven to put the coffee on.

This morning, she was tired and stayed in bed. He had slipped out of the bedroom, made his own coffee and sat on the porch.

What he hated most of all since retiring, was that the consistent event in his life was funerals. There seemed to be one every month. There was one this morning. That was the reason for his early rising. He had another funeral to go to. It wasn't even a friend. It was a one time workmate who he vaguely remembered.

He looked at the photo of the man in the obituary, he looked familiar, but age had taken so much. Ben...Ben something. He checked the name. Ben Moore? It didn't ring a bell. Maybe he never knew his last name. Hell, perhaps he didn't know him at all. He had worked for nearly forty years at the company and could think of only six people he knew. Six! Of the over two hundred employees in the office he had worked at, and he could think of only six.

The dead man looked tired, tired and old. Everyone looked so old.

A couple of weeks ago they had gone to the funeral of a classmate from high school. The photo that had been placed on the easel was of a smiling, happy fat old woman with bad hair. He had looked at the face, trying to find the girl he had known in high school. He hadn't had any success.

He had walked in. A lot of people had been standing around, talking quietly. He'd recognized no one. In the corner were several cork boards with photos from her life. He walked to them.

She had had a nice life. Nothing fancy, just a life; laughter and smiles, a husband, kids, grandkids. All the things you are supposed to have to be happy. Now she was dead.

Later that afternoon, back at home sitting on his porch, he pulled out his yearbooks and looked for her. When he found her, he was surprised. He had known her. They had actually dated. How had he forgotten? As he stared at the small black-and-white photo of her, memories came back to him. She had been so cute, a tiny, shy blonde with a habit of looking through her hair. He had found it very exciting. He looked at her photo for a long time. Moments with her drifted in his mind. They'd had some fun.

He looked at her photo on the funeral program. He stared hard at the face, a round plump wrinkled face. Yes, she was there. In her eyes, he found her, lost in her wrinkles. He stared at her eyes, remembering moments that he had shared with that sweet young girl.

He cried then. Cried for a thing lost. He cried for a thing he didn't even really know he had had. Frustrated with himself, he angrily wiped the tears away. He looked around to see if anyone had seen him cry. No one had. The street was empty. He stared at the photo, then he flipped to his own yearbook photo. There he was, so young, so timid, so skinny.

Had he changed as much as she had? He rose and went into the house. In the bathroom, he stared at his face. No, he was there. He could still see himself. Then he looked back at the yearbook photo of himself. With a shock, he realized he was unrecognizable as that young man. He had changed that much. Gravity and fat had rendered him unrecognizable. His face swelled and had been pulled down. If he was honest with himself, he looked like a melted apple head.

His back spasmed. Wincing, he groaned in pain. He had

been leaning forward over the sink too long. Hands on his lower back, eyes pressed shut, he slowly straightened.

The yearbook slid off the vanity to the floor. He resisted the impulse to catch it. He knew to reach for it would cause him pain for the next couple of weeks. Instead, he watched the book slip to the floor, landing face up.

"Youandus," it read. He had never understood what it meant until that very moment.

"Oh shit. You and Us. That's what it says." All these years, he hadn't known.

He walked painfully back to his porch and sat heavily in his chair, and looked at the street. It seemed he had watched it forever.

"I hate being old," he said to the street and felt guilty for saying it. His dad's words came to him.

Be grateful for getting older. Many people don't get that gift.

He wondered if he was grateful when he died in a dirty, run-down old folks' home in wet diapers, unable to recognize anyone, being fed baby food by a surly woman who hated her job and took it out on him. Was he grateful to still be alive then?

Every other week he would go to visit his father in the home he had found for him. He felt it was duty as a son. He would sit and talk about his life, what was happening and what he was planning. The last time he was there, he had yammered on. Then he stopped. What was the point? He sat looking at what had been his father, now a smelly drooling nothing. He stood and left. He didn't look back, and he never returned. A few months later, he got a call that his dad had passed away.

He had walked through the preparations, the funeral and the wake, never crying, never even feeling sad. For him, the funeral was just a much-belated formality. His dad had died many years before.

He looked at the empty cup in his hand. He looked at the dead street and considered if he wanted another cup. No, it would just make for a long night. He put the cup on the deck beside him.

He looked at the empty street. Far off, a woman walked past being pulled by a dog. His neighbour three doors down came out in a robe for the paper. The neighbour's legs were very pale and skinny.

He stood slowly, his hip complained, as it always did. Turning to go in, he remembered his empty coffee cup. Bending to pick it up, he felt his back spasm, and the pain hit him. He winced and decided he could leave the cup for now. He turned back to the door.

It was horribly quiet in the house. There was a time when quiet was wonderful. It had been something he sought. A time he wished for and could only find treasured minutes to cling to. Now it was a terrible thing. It surrounded him, an all-consuming void. It hung off him like a heavy, wet blanket. It pushed him down, forcing all the air from his lungs and made his breath come in short, shallow gasps.

He moved through the dark, silent house. Only the squeaks and groans of the old floorboards broke the quiet, and then only enough to make the quiet worse.

A thought had crossed his mind. Somewhere he had a box his wife had squirrelled away, full of photos. He was sure he knew where she had put it. An hour later, he was still looking. He had run out of places to look. Now he was revisiting closets and drawers, some for the third or even fourth time.

He stood in their bedroom and looked at her, the blanket tight up to her chin; he tried to imagine where she would have put it. He walked back to the first place he had looked, the closet in their bedroom and there it was. The box he had spent an hour looking for was right there. How had he not seen it? He pulled it down and quietly left the room.

In the kitchen, he made himself another coffee in a fresh mug. He took the coffee and the box of photos out to the porch. He sat. The view hadn't changed much, a little activity, but not much. This had always been a quiet street.

He took a sip and opened the box. In this box was his life broken into stills separated by months, sometimes by years, and in no order. He put the box down, pulled out a handful of photos and sat back.

The first was a square black and white print, of him and his wife on a beach somewhere. He was holding her; she had her back pressed against him. She was smiling at him with that smile he knew so well. He remembered the photo, but he couldn't remember the time. He stared at it, his wife would remember. She always did.

He put the photo aside and looked at the next. This one was a Polaroid, its colour bright, almost garish. It was out of focus, but he remembered its story. It was a photo of him and his best friend on a fishing trip. It had been a wonderful holiday, just the two of them. He smiled at the memory, trying to remember what lake they had gone to.

Wait, they hadn't gone alone. Who took the photo? Then he realized who the third person had been. He was...what was his name? It was a plain name. John? Yes, John.

A flood of memories came to him, and he remembered what he had worked hard to forget. The day that photo had been taken was the last day of their fishing trip. They had been laughing and drinking. They had closed up camp, and John had driven off on his own. He never made it home. He had

26

lost control of his car on a corner, smashing into the side of a logging truck. He died there.

How had he forgotten? He had felt so guilty. They had been drinking. He had pushed for one last drink, one last drink. He pushed the photo back in the box and looked at the next. This one was creased. It was an old photo, sepia and faded, with scalloped edges.

It was of himself, maybe 15 or 16, down on one knee, his arms around a big German Shepherd. It was Hunter, his best friend for many years. They had been inseparable. He was with him when he discovered girls, and was there when he got his heart broken, but it was Hunter who truly broke his heart. It wasn't long after this photo was taken, Hunter stopped eating. His hips were hurting him, and he no longer wanted to go out in the fields. Gramma said that it was time. He hadn't understood at first.

"You don't want him ta suffer, do ya?" she had asked.

"No."

"Well, grampa's got a lead pill for him. He won't be hurtin' no more. You just stay here with me, an' grampa will take ol' Hunter fer a walk."

He never saw Hunter again. His gramma gave him some static about crying.

"Get over it. It's jus' a dog. Man up," she said.

He had never stopped thinking about Hunter. He looked at the photo for a long time.

Hours passed, with each photo he fell into the past. He was amazed at the events that came to him. So many people he had forgotten. So many things that had happened that he had not thought about in years, some good, some bad.

Some memories he had that he told people about were wrong. He had been telling about events that hadn't happened the way he remembered. They had changed sometimes in small ways, like in that game 'broken telephone', others he wasn't even sure had happened at all.

He wove through his past, each photo pulling him one way then another. When he looked up, the sun was low. The day had slid by unnoticed.

He put the photos away and sat back in his chair. He took a sip of his now cold coffee. Staring at the street, he felt a sadness settled on him. It wasn't a new thing. It had always been there, just a step away, just a thought away. A shadow he had pushed back all his life.

Now it came to him, heavy and thick. Knowledge that entered his mind and broke him. His life could have been so much more. He always took the safe route, always. Every step had been about what his parents thought, what his friends thought, and never what he thought, what he wanted.

He looked at the street, nearly dark now. Soon the streetlights will come on. It was getting cooler.

He pushed himself to his feet. It was time to go in. He picked up the box of photos, looked at the coffee cups, turned and went inside, leaving them where they were.

The house was quiet. He thought of his wife, all tucked in. He put the photos down on the coffee table and went upstairs. There was still a tiny amount of light coming in the bedroom window. It was the end of magic hour, that time of golden light. The street bathed in the dying sun. It looked as good as it ever did, awash in the gold. He smiled at the sight.

He looked down at his wife, pushed a hair from her forehead and adjusted the blanket. Her forehead was cool. He turned the thermostat up.

In the bathroom, he took care of his nightly routine.

When he returned to the bedroom, it was dark outside. The room had warmed some.

He smiled as he crawled into bed with his wife, happy to join her. He still loved her after all these years. He spooned her, and with a sigh, he closed his eyes.

# CHAPTER 3

## PASSING IT FORWARD

Usually, all ten of the motel's windows facing Highway 11 had the drapes closed tight against the headlights of westbound cars that glared straight into those rooms making it nearly impossible to sleep. There weren't many cars passing. This stretch of blacktop was rarely used, but even one could ruin a night's sleep.

Glen stood in the frozen gravel drive off Highway 11, his back to the motel, looking into the dark forest across the highway. Behind him, a single light on a pole lit the parking area. It cast a long shadow in front of him into the dark.

He considered his breath as it frosted in the night air. It mixed with the smoke from his cigarette. He took a drag, then flicked the butt into the dark and watched the glowing tip vanish. His jacket was open, despite the cold. He could feel its bite on his nose and fingertips.

He looked into the sky above him. He was always amazed at how many stars he could see here. In the city there were stars, but here there were a thousand times more. Tonight however, the sky was dark. The stars were nowhere to be seen and the moon shone weakly through heavy cloud cover.

He turned and looked at the motel. The motel must have been sitting here for over 40 years, maybe longer, and it showed. He had started working here when he had dropped out of college. He didn't want to go back home and hear the disappointment in his mother's voice again. A friend in his dorm had said he knew of a job that would pay OK, and it would give him a quiet place to consider what he was going to do next.

It certainly gave him time to think. Every night for the past three months, he sat at the desk and read and thought and smoked. He wasn't any closer to an idea than the day he'd arrived. He had begun to believe this had been a bad idea. This motel had started to feel like a prison, like a place he would never escape.

It wasn't a busy motel. Many nights, he had not one stop. A person had to be pretty tired to stop here. It wasn't welcoming. It needed paint. The office window was cracked, with a small sliver of glass missing. Years ago, someone had taped the hole over with masking tape. The tape had all but disintegrated.
'Motel' written in big block letters on the roof, had a horror movie feel. Many of the bulbs that shone up at the wooden painted letters were burnt out or on their last days. The tiny neon 'office' sign was barely visible.

He looked at the single black window. It reminded him of a missing tooth. It was the second to last window. It was room nine. He wanted to go and check, yet he also did not want to. He was unsure of what he would find. He would have to check soon, but not yet. He stared at the black window. With an animal shake he walked back to his office.

He sat in his chair and stared out the window. Nights were quiet. He had been on the nightshift from day one. The owner of the motel had asked if he was OK with the night shift. Glen had said it was perfect. He needed time to think. The man had laughed, "Well, you'll get plenty of time for that," and hired him.

Glen pulled out his Jack Reacher novel that he had found in a used bookstore. It was dog-eared and had cost him a buck. He had read it before, but enjoyed the security of a world where one man could be that sure, that untroubled by anything. He read and reread the same paragraph, and in frustration, he put the book down. He leaned back in his chair. It creaked and threatened to tip over backwards. He was doing his best not to think about room nine, not to think about what was in there.

He sat for as long as he could. He put the 'Back in a minute' sign on the window and walked down the building. He stood looking at the door with the 9 on it.

He knocked lightly, then opened the door. It was dark in the room except for the light that came in from the yard.

"Hello?" he whispered to the dark. There was no response. The bathroom door opened, and light flooded out. A dream walked out, carried by the light. He stared, his mouth open. She was a vision, a vision out of his deepest fantasy.

The woman stood, unselfconsciously naked except for a towel around her head. She smiled at him.

"Hello," she said. She pulled the towel off and bent forward to dry her hair.

"Are you OK?" he asked.

"I'm fine. Much better, thank you, and thank you for letting me stay here."

"Humm, no problem," he said, "I don't have any clothes that would fit you, but I brought you a pair of coveralls."

"Oh, thank you. That's great." She stepped forward and took the rolled-up bundle. They were used and smelled of oil and varsol. She unrolled the coveralls, stepped into the legs and pulled them over her shoulders.

He should look away. He shouldn't stare, but he couldn't pull away. He was mesmerized.

Her ribs pushed up and forward as she pulled her arms into the sleeves. She bent and rolled up the long pant legs, first one leg, then the other. Once done, she stood straight and started rolling up the sleeves. The zipper still undone opened; one breast teased him as it popped in and out of view.

Once her sleeves were rolled up, she pulled the zipper up to her neck. He felt a pang of loss.

"You should close the curtains," he said, pointing at them.

She looked at him, puzzled and said, "OK." She walked past him and closed the curtains.

"Do you need anything? Are you hungry?" he asked.

"No, I don't think so," she responded. Again the puzzled look.

"You look a lot better," he said.

"I do?"

Now it was his turn to look puzzled.

He remembered how he had found her. He had slipped out back for a smoke, and she had been laying in the snow. The snow was stained red from the blood. Her clothing was shredded, and was mostly torn away as was her flesh. She was drenched with blood.

He was sure she was dead, then her eyes flashed open.

He went to her. He didn't know what to do. She looked bad. He reached for her but stopped, afraid to touch her.

"It's OK. I'll call an ambulance."

"NO!" she said and had grabbed his hand with such force it had hurt.

"But you're hurt!" he said looking around, trying to decide what to do.

"It's not as bad as it looks. I just need a place to clean up and maybe sleep," she said. She rolled slightly to her left and pushed herself upright. He rushed forward and helped her to her feet. She was tiny. He held her up and walked her to the closest room.

He opened the room and switched on the light. She flinched and screamed, "NO, no light."

"OK, OK," he said, turning the light off. He had seen her though, in that brief light, had seen deep gashes across her back and chest that were still bleeding. She was cut up pretty badly.

He winced as he lay her down on the bed, partly from the pain it caused her and partly from the blood that was certainly going to be soaking into the bedding. He wasn't sure how he was going to explain that.

She whimpered, curled into a fetal pose and fell asleep. He stood, looking at her. He really should call the cops or something. This was nuts. He was in so much trouble. Her hand reached out and grasped his.

"Thank you. Just a little time. It will all be OK," she said.

She held his hand. He stood still for a long time, her hand slipped as she fell into a deeper sleep. He watched her breathing. It was rhythmic and steady. He turned and left for a smoke.

Remembering this, he exclaimed, "You were all cut up when I found you."

She looked at him, "Oh, that. It looked far worse than it was," she smiled.

"It looked pretty bad. You had very deep gashes on your back and your chest. I saw them," he said, suddenly not as sure as he had been a few minutes ago.

"Well, you just saw me," she smiled, tipping her head down slightly, "I looked alright, didn't I?"

"Yes," he said, blushing.

She smiled, enjoying his discomfort. She sat on the edge of the bed.

"What happened to you?" he asked.

Her smile slipped, then returned as bright as ever.

"Oh, it was a misunderstanding. My father..."

"Wait! Your dad did that to you?" he said, shocked.

"No... well, not really," she looked down at her hands, "It was not his fault."

"What do you mean? Did he do this?"

"Well, what he did, he didn't know he did. He didn't know what he gave me, and that was a while ago. 'Sides, he bit a lead pill a couple of months back, so it's not important anymore," she laughed lightly, "I guess it wasn't lead. A silver pill then," she smiled at her private joke.

He looked at her, baffled by how she could defend her dad if he was responsible for what he had seen.

"Glen, right?" She stood and moved close to him.

"Um, yes, Glen," he said.

She moved closer still, "I need you to help me, Glen." She put her hand on his chest, "I need a place to stay for a couple of days."

"I...you can't stay here. I'm sorry. My shift ends at six."

"I just need a couple of days. Can I come home with you?" She slid her arm up and around his neck, "Just a couple of days."

"It's not much," he said, thinking about the small house he rented. It was tiny.

"It will be perfect," she pulled him down to her and kissed him.

"I guess you can come," he mumbled.

She kissed him again, jumped, wrapped her legs around him.

He returned her smile.

"But first I have to clean up this room," he said, looking about.

"I can help," she said brightly.

The comforter was soaked with blood. There was a single small barefoot print in blood on the carpet. He wasn't sure what he was going to do about that, but the comforter and the sheets he could replace from the storeroom. He couldn't leave them with laundry. There would be questions. He would take them home, wash them at his laundromat and return them clean.

He looked at her. He realized he didn't know her name.

"What's your name?"

She laughed, "Christine, Christine Rutland. Nice to meet you." She extended her small hand. He smiled and shook it.

"You stay here, Christine. It's too cold to be traipsing around in bare feet. I'll go and get clean bedding," he said.

He hesitated, wondering if leaving her alone was such a good idea, then–still unsure–turned and left. The storeroom was behind the office. He walked through the cold, unlocked the storeroom and pulled the chain to turn the light on. He had to slide around the maid's cart to the bedding. He pulled down sheets, pillowcases, and a comforter. He pulled the chain, locked the door and walked back. He glanced at his watch. Still an hour before his shift ended.

He opened the door to nine and stopped. Christine was on her hands and knees in the middle of the floor. At first, he could not figure out what she was doing, then he saw. She was licking the bloody footprint.

"What...?" he asked. He couldn't believe what he was seeing.

She sat back on her heels and smiled at him. She wiped her mouth with a hand.

"I've just about got it all," she said with pride.

He looked at the carpet. She was right, it was gone. "Gross," he thought, "but it worked."

Slightly shaken, he moved to the bed and pulled the comforter off. Christine rose and helped. It was done in minutes. Glen rolled up the bloody bedding.

"Stay here. I'll be right back," he said.

"Oh, just a sec," she ran to the bathroom and came back holding what remained of her clothes.

"Don't forget these." She held them out with two fingers and screwed up her nose. He took the blood-soaked rags, once again marvelling at how much blood she had lost yet had no wounds on her at all.

He took the bedding and rags to his truck and tossed them into the box. He leaned on the truck. This wasn't right. He looked up at the sky, looking for stars, but saw only black. A quick glance at his watch. Dave would be here soon to take over. He climbed into the truck and started it. It took a couple of turns before it fired but then roared to life. He turned the heater on high and closed the door, letting it idle.

He walked back to the room. Christine was sitting on the

bed. She looked up when he came in and smiled. Glen looked around the room. It looked OK.

"Dave will be here soon. I'll take you to the truck. It'll be warm. You can wait there," he said.

"OK," she said and stood.

"Your feet will freeze. I'll carry you." He stepped forward. She smiled at him and put her arms around his neck, "OK," she whispered.

He picked her up easily and carried her to his truck. She opened the door, and he lifted her to the truck seat. It wasn't warm, but it was getting there.

He had closed the truck door and started walking to the office when he saw headlights on the highway. The car slowed, signalled, and turned into the parking lot. It was Dave, slightly early as always. He pulled his Ford up to the office, shut it off and stepped out.

"Morning," Glen said.

Dave looked at him, frowned, "Morning."

Dave wasn't a morning person. He needed several cups of coffee and about an hour to come alive.

"Nothing has changed. Only those two guys from the plant in 11 and 12," Glen said.

"K," Dave responded as he walked to the office, Glen following. Glen watched Dave hang up his coat, sit and adjust things the way he liked them. He handed Glen his dog-eared paperback with a look of distaste.

"Ok. Have a good morning," Dave said.

"You too," Glen said as he left the office.

Glen walked to his truck, his boots squeaking in the snow. It always seemed colder just before dawn. The cab was warm when he climbed in. Christine smiled at him. She waited till he had settled into his seat, then she slid across the seat to sit right beside him. It made him feel special.

The truck was an old standard Chev with the long stick that stood straight from the floorboards. He pulled the stick back into reverse. His fingers stroked her thigh. She pushed forward into his fingers. His body reacted like he had never felt before. For a second, he was flustered, confusion washing over him.

He shook slightly and pushed the truck into first, and pulled out onto the highway.

Glen had rented a cabin not far from the motel. They were only a few minutes on the highway when Christine pulled her legs up, slid down her head in Glen's lap and fell asleep. Overwhelmed by the coveralls, she looked like a child. Glen looked at her quiet, sleeping face. He felt a swell of a feeling he was unfamiliar with. He needed to protect her. He needed to keep her safe.

When he got to the cabin, she was still asleep. He picked her up easily and carried her into the cabin. The cabin was usually rented to hunters and ice fisherman in the winter months, and in the summer to families on vacation. It was small, but it had all he needed: a kitchen, a bedroom and a bathroom with a shower. It didn't have much in the way of hot water, but enough. In the main room was a small potbelly stove.

He put her down on the old blue couch and set to lighting a fire in the stove. The cabin warmed quickly. He made his bed, then sat down beside her on the couch to wait for her to wake. He woke in bed. A sliver of sunlight edged his heavy curtains. He stretched, then jumped when a soft voice said, "Afternoon, sleepyhead. You want a coffee?"

He sat up, the night before flooding back. Christine sat at the edge of his bed, smiling.

"Ya, a coffee would be great."

Christine stood and skipped out of the room. She was wearing one of his sweaters. It hung off one shoulder and halfway down to her knees.

She came back in a minute, smiling, carrying a mug. He took it in both hands.

"Thank you," he said, "I musta been very tired. I don't remember comin' to bed."

"Oh, honey. When I woke, you were passed out. You looked so cute." She touched his cheek, "So I put you to bed."

"I don't remember," he sipped on his coffee.

"You never woke. I carried you in and tucked you in."

He looked down, noticing he was naked under the covers.

"Ya, I tucked you in. I thought you would be more comfortable without all those tight clothes." She grinned, as he looked down. Her eyes looked at him from under her eyebrows. There was mischief in those eyes.

"You undressed me?" he asked.

"After I carried you in here," she smiled, her head coming up.

"Wait. What do you mean, 'You' carried me?"

"I'm stronger than I look," she said proudly.

He looked at her, surprised.

She leaned forward. The sweater hung open, revealing her small breasts. He looked. She smiled as she took his coffee, placed it on the night table, and pulled the sweater over her head.

She stood in front of him naked. He looked at her. Inside, he laughed at himself. Here is this gorgeous woman standing naked in front of him, and he's looking for half-healed cuts or scars. There was nothing. Her skin was perfect. She was perfect.

Christine climbed into bed, pushing him back and down. "See? Nothing. Not a scratch. I heal quick." she said and kissed him.

When he woke, he was alone. The slit at the side of his curtain showed nothing but dark. He glanced at his watch. It was after 8.

"Christine?" he called. He pushed the sheets down and went to the bathroom. While he was pissing, he caught his reflection in the vanity mirror. He had long scratches down his back. He reached around, touched them, winced and smiled at how he had gotten them.

"Christine?" He called louder this time. He walked around the small cabin looking for her, knowing she was gone. Somewhere deep inside himself, a little thing broke like a tiny spring that he never knew existed, suddenly gave under a lifetime of strain.

He walked to the window and pushed open the curtain. He looked at the snow-draped forest in the semi-dark. He stood till the sun had set and he could see the reflection of his naked pale body. He looked at himself. He was just a man, nothing special. She was special, out of this world special. A being so pure it could never belong to someone like him.

He turned from the window and got dressed. It would soon be time to go to work. But it wasn't. He had hours to wait and nothing to fill them with. He sat on his couch as the cabin cooled. The fire had died long ago. He knew he should restart the fire. He knew he should eat something. He sat staring at nothing, until it was time to go.

He pulled on his coat and boots, and trudged to the truck. He groaned when he realized he had forgotten to plug it in. The truck barely turned over. At first he was sure it wouldn't start but finally with a roar it came to life. His breath white in the cab, he drove to the motel and fell into his routine. His shift passed without excitement.

On his drive home, an idea popped into his mind. Maybe she's there waiting for me.

He pushed hard on the accelerator. His old truck growled as it shifted down. He skidded into the campsite and stopped in front of his cabin, threw the truck door open and raced to the door. Inside, it was cold and dark. She was not there.

He stood in the middle of the room. He walked to the couch and sat. After a couple of minutes, he laid down. His coat still on, he pulled his booted feet up on the couch and fell asleep.

"Glen?" The voice was a man's, coming from outside. Glen heard it. He ignored it. He was tired. He just needed to sleep.

"Glen?" The voice was closer, then the voice was right beside him.

"Glen! What the fuck! You gonna freeze!" he yelled, shaking Glen. He pulled Glen to a sitting position, "Wake up!"

"I'm tired. Just let me sleep," Glen said or thought he had. It came out as unintelligible mumbles.

"Glen! Wake up!" the man yelled again. He shook Glen. "Fuck! Ah gotta warm you up!"

He rushed to the stove, slamming the door shut as he passed. He got the fire burning, went to the kitchen and turned on the elements and oven, leaving the oven door open. He raced around the cottage, opening the curtains to let in the sunlight. Glen had slid back down to a prone position. The man sat him upright again.

"Glen! Wake up! You can't sleep now!" the man yelled. Glen tried to push the man away. He felt drunk, his movements clumsy. The man slapped him across the face, hard. His eyes popped open, startled.

"What..?" Glen managed to say.

It took some work, but the man finally got Glen on his feet. He stumbled around with the man's arms helping. They walked till the man was sweating and Glen was moving on his own. The cabin was warm.

Glen recognized his saviour. It was Sam, the old guy he had rented the cabin from.

"I saw yer truck with the door open, then I saw the cabin door open too. What the fuck were you thinking?" Sam asked.

Glen looked at Sam, "I was just tired. It was a long shift."

"Well, pretty fucking stupid," he said. He looked around the cabin. "Ok, you ok?"

"Ya, I'm good. Thank you," Glen said. Sam grunted and left. Glen shut off the stove and oven. He undressed, had a warm shower till the water became cold, crawled into bed and went to sleep.

It was night when he woke. He hadn't drawn the curtains, and the blackness surrounded the cabin. He slipped out of bed, hugged himself against the chill of the air and put some wood in the stove. It was down to embers, but it got burning quickly.

He went to the window to look at the stars through the trees. He could see very few because the moon, full and bright, dominated the sky. He looked at the moon, it seemed so close.

In the cold night air, it had an intensity that seemed to almost have a heat to it. He felt a pull to it like vertigo.

A shape caught his eye as he was looking up. It crossed the yard between the cabin and his truck. The moonlight outlined the shape. He wasn't sure what it was, an animal, maybe a dog or bear. It was dark, fur-covered and moved quickly past the truck into the trees where it vanished. It could have been anything. He was living in the boonies.

He turned back to the room. He checked his watch. It was nearly time to go to work. He crossed the floor, dressed, pulled on his coat and boots.

Outside, he looked for tracks in the snow. He found too many to decipher anything from them.

Once again, he had forgotten to plug the truck in. He turned the ignition, and was rewarded with a dull click. He tried a couple more times. He was going to need a boost. He plugged the truck in knowing it wouldn't do much good at this point, and if he wasn't going to be late, he'd have to walk over to Sam's. Late as it was, he hoped Sam was in, awake, and willing to come out to give him a boost.

His feet crunched on the cold hard-packed snow. He shoved his hands deep in his pockets, hunched over against the cold. The hairs in his nose seemed to freeze. It took a few minutes to get to Sam's. Glen was happy to see that the house was lit up.

A noise off to his right in the trees made him turn. Something was following him, walking in the deep snow there. He walked faster. The footfalls didn't speed up, but neither did they stop.

He was nearly running by the time he got to Sam's front door. Whatever was pacing him had stopped, he could no longer hear it in the trees. He knocked on Sam's door and heard Sam curse from inside. The door flew open, Sam stood in the doorway glaring but softened when he recognized Glen.

"Oh, it's you. You OK?" Sam asked.

"Yes, I'm good. Thanks again. That was stupid," Glen said.

"It sure the fuck was," Sam said, "What do you need?"

"I'm sorry to bug you with this but my truck. I didn't plug it in so..."

"So, you need a boost. OK, no problem. Step inside while I get my coat an' boots on." Sam turned from the door, leaving it open for Glen to walk in. He followed, glancing behind at the trees. He didn't see anything.

Sam's house was nothing like his cabins, it was a real home. From where Glen stood watching Sam pull his jacket on, he could see Sam's wife. He couldn't remember her name. The room she was in was dark except for the glow of the TV.

"I'm going to give Glen a boost," Sam called out.

"K. Is he OK?" Sam's wife asked.

"I'm good, thanks," Glen said.

"I'm glad to hear it. Stay warm,"

"Back in a sec," Sam said as he opened the door to his right that led to the garage. Glen followed, closing the door behind him.

It only took a minute to drive back to Glen's truck. Sam nosed in tight to it. They got out, opened their hoods and hooked up the cables that Sam had pulled from behind the seat. Glen climbed into the cab and the engine started after a few tries. He left it idling, jumped out to help but Sam had the cables unhooked and rolled up already.

"Thanks, Sam. You're a lifesaver."

"Yup, more than once," Sam smiled. "Don't make it ah habit."

"No'ser. I won't," Glen chuckled.

Glen climbed into the cab of his truck as Sam drove away. It was already warming up. He drove to work, his mind on Christine. He had so many questions. He couldn't stop thinking about her.

He got to the motel and settled into his shift. He picked up his book again. He put it down when he had reread the same paragraph three times and still couldn't remember what it was about. He just couldn't concentrate. He stared into the night and shivered. It was so cold and dark. To be out in that, alone and hurt. It terrified him.

Something moved just out of sight, a slightly less dark shape against the black. He stood and looked harder. There was something there.

He pulled his coat on, grabbed a flashlight and walked outside. He pointed the flashlight's beam into the black past the parking lot's light. It found nothing. He kept moving forward till he reached the edge of the light. The flashlight beam pushed against the dark.

Two red dots in the black. He stared, not knowing what he was looking at, then the red dots blinked. Glen stepped back a pace. The red eyes stared at him, steadily, calmly. He took another step backwards. From the dark, he heard a low growl. So low, so slow it was a series of bass note clicks. He stopped. He realized that the animal he was looking at was either very large or in a tree. The eyes were more than a head taller than himself. He hoped it was in a tree. The growl came again, so low he felt it rather than heard it. He stepped backwards.

The creature stepped forward, the moonlight catching the top of its head. It was not a small creature in a tree. Its large triangular head could just be seen. It had very tall pointed

47

ears with tufts of hair at the tips making them look even taller, thinner.

He stood still, eyes wide, mouth agape. When the growl came again, he turned and ran.

He ran flat out like a hound from hell was on his tail... and maybe it was. He tripped in the middle of the parking lot. He fell hard skidding on the frozen gravel. He rolled onto his back, expecting fangs to snatch at him, claws to tear at him.

Nothing. No claws, no fangs and no red eyes. Only the dark.

Suddenly the air was filled with a roar, and brightness surrounded him. He crabbed backwards as a truck skidded to a stop, narrowly missing him. The driver jumped out of the truck.

"What the hell are ya doin on the ground! I damn near run ya over!" the driver yelled.

Glen looked past the driver, to the dark of the forest.

"What's wrong with you? Ya drunk or sumin?"

"No, no, sorry. Just slipped," Glen said.

"Well, it's a good way to got yer self kilt."

The black mass that flew out of the dark, smashed into the driver with such force it lifted the side of the truck up, threatening to tip it over and pushing it sideways several feet. The driver had enough time to scream once, then the inside of the truck's windshield was hosed with blood. The truck shook violently as sounds of rending and tearing, mixed with low snarling, filled the parking lot.

Glen scrambled to his feet and raced to the office. He slammed the door behind himself and grabbed the phone, and dialled 911.

"This is Glen at the motel on 89. There's a wolf or a bear attacking a man in the parking lot!"

From where Glen stood, phone to his ear, only partly

hearing the woman on the other end of the line saying they were sending someone, he watched the truck shake. He stopped listening completely when the truck went still. His arm sank, still holding the receiver.

From around the truck stepped a wolf, but unlike any wolf he had ever seen. It had huge hackles, long ears and a thin tapering snout. Its red eyes looked at him. It was tall, standing taller than he was, on surprisingly thin, almost delicate legs that ended in large paws. It stood still for what seemed like a long time, then its ears perked. Its lips pulled back to reveal extremely long canines. It growled low and turned to disappear into the dark trees.

Glen stood still for several minutes until he heard sirens coming down the highway. He became aware he still held the receiver at his side. He brought it to his ear. The woman was frantic.

"Yes," he said calmly and hung up.

The two cop cars came screaming into the parking lot seconds later. The blue and red flashing lights bathed the parking lot in a weird festive atmosphere. He walked out of his office, slow and calm.

"You Glen?" the young cop called.

"Yes," Glen said as he walked towards him.

"Where's the attack?"

"Yes," Glen said pointing at the truck.

He watched two of the officers walk to the truck. They both swore when they saw what was there. One gagged but didn't throw up. The remaining two officers nervously joined them. They turned on Glen, demanding to know what happened. He told them, calm and detached, then he told them again.

More cops arrived as well as an ambulance. It was crowded.

Absently Glen thought he wasn't going to have any customers tonight. His boss would be pissed. It wasn't his fault, he thought indignantly.

He overheard one of the cops who seemed to be in charge complaining, "This is the worst fucking day! Starting with some young girl going on a killing spree with a kitchen knife. Sliced up her boyfriend, now this. I fucking hate full moons. It brings on the crazy."

Glen was asked several more times what he had seen. By the time they said he could go home, the sun was up. His boss was stomping around trying to get this mess cleaned up as soon as possible so he could get back to business. He wasn't having much luck. He didn't talk to Glen, just nodded.

Glen drove to his cabin slowly. Pulled up in front. Plugged the truck in as he walked to his door. Inside he walked straight to his bed, crawled in fully dressed and went to sleep.

It was late afternoon when he awoke to a noise. He climbed out of bed and walked into the main room. Christine sat there on the couch in his dirty, too big coveralls.

"Christine?" he said.

She looked at him. There was a sadness in her eyes, "Hi, Glen. Miss me?"

"Christine, where'd you go?"

She shook her head. "Oh, I've been around."

He wanted to go to her, to pick her up, to hold her, but something in her voice made him stay where he was.

"I'm sorry. I thought I could do it. I thought I could stay away. You are so kind, so loving, and it's not fair, but I like you." She stood, stepping towards him. "My father didn't know what he did. He thought he was doing what he had to. He was wrong, but I never got to tell him."

She stopped in the middle of the room and glanced out the window at the creeping twilight.

"I don't want to be alone. My last boyfriend wasn't nice to me when the change came over him. I fixed him earlier today." She smiled and started to unzip the coveralls, "I want you to be with me. I'm sorry there is only one way you and I can be together."

She let the coveralls fall to the floor. She stood in the half-light, beautiful, pale and naked. Glen's eyes traced her body. He felt himself stir.

Something shifted. It must be the failing light. She looked taller. She jerked, then she bent over like she was in pain. Her long hair fell forward. The light slipped into darkness. She growled low. When she stood, two red eyes regarded him. He stood frozen, trying to understand what had just happened.

She leaped.

He said and stretched out his arms as wide as he could, relishing the feel of them.

# CHAPTER 4

## HAYMAKER

The blow came out of nowhere, a a massive strike to the head, bone-deep. He felt it all the way through his skull to the other side, like a piece of the earth had come up and slammed into his jaw. It rattled his brain, and shook his eyes. He saw stars. His teeth ground against each other. He couldn't see, couldn't think. Everything stopped in a flash of blinding white.

He stepped back a couple paces, arms windmilling. He righted himself, tasting iron. He felt warmth under his nose. He wiped the back of his hand across his upper lip and wasn't surprised to see blood. He bent forward, crouched and ready.

His fists balled; his legs braced. He lunged, swinging a huge wide-swinging punch aimed to end the fight. He missed.

Jacob pulled back just enough, jabbed, catching Brian straight in the face. Brian heard and felt his nose crunch. A sickening sound he had heard once before, at Jacob's fist. His eyes watered, blinding him for a second.

Every year it was the same thing. Brian and Jacob were the best of friends until they weren't. A boiling point would be reached, and the release was their annual fight, one Brian inevitably lost. After the fight, in a week or so, they would be friends again till next year.

This year was different.

This year Jacob had done something so incredibly stupid Brian couldn't leave it be. Jacob's decision was not only stupid, it scared Brian.

Brian wouldn't admit it now, but he loved Jacob and what Jacob had done changed everything. It changed who Brian saw Jacob as, it made Jacob not the man he thought he was.

It was fucking stupid. To sell your soul to the Judge was beyond stupid, beyond anything like stupid, and for what? A truck. A TRUCK! FER FUCK SAKE!

Brian swung again. Another wild haymaker. This time, Jacob stood his ground. His fist collided with Jacob's hard head. There was a loud crunch. Brian yelped, grabbing his hand. Jacob smiled, looking at Brian, whose face had gone white.

"Are we done?" Jacob asked. Brian was bent over his hand, clutched against his stomach, moaning. "Ya, we're done," Jacob turned and walked away.

The gathered crowd groaned, hoping for an epic beat down. This was just sad.

Brian sank to his knees, his pale forehead touched the grass. He was sure he had broken his hand. He stayed that way for several minutes, then he sat back on his heels. He was alone in the field.

Slowly he stood and went to the nurse's station. There would be hell to pay for fighting on school grounds, but he needed someone to look at his hand.

He was right. The principal yelled, and Brian waited. Finally, after it was obvious Brian wasn't going to tell him who he had been fighting with, the principal left.

An hour later, he was back in class with a soft cast halfway up his forearm. He hadn't broken anything, just severely bruised, but he had a story to tell.

For the rest of the afternoon, he laughed and told anyone who would listen about the fight.

After school, Jacob walked up to Brian, sitting on the school's front step, waiting for the bus that would take him home. "How's the hand?" Jacob asked, sitting down on the step beside Brian.

"Ah, it's fine. You got one fucking hard head."

"Ya, bin told that afore," he laughed, "Sides my deal makes me a bit harder."

"Yer deal, huh." Brian frowned, "Give me a ride home."

"Ya sure. Com'on."

They stood and walked to the parking lot. Jacob's brand new 1977 Chevy half-ton, Clyde, was there shining in the afternoon sun.

"That's a fine truck." Brian said, then noticed a sizable dent in Clyde's front fender, "Hey, what the fuck. There's a dint in the fender! Somebody hit you?"

"Ya. You did that," Jacob chuckled.

"The hell I did!" Brian said, "I never touched Clyde."

"No, but that last punch landed hard."

"Ah don't get it." Brian looked at the fist-sized dent in Clyde's front fender.

"It's part of my deal. I get hit. Clyde here takes the damage fer me. It's great."

"What the fuck!" Brian said.

"An' the best part, Clyde here heals. That dint will be gone by morn," Jacob smiled.

Brian looked at Jacob then back to Clyde, "OK, that's fucked up," he said, shaking his head.

He walked around the truck and pulled open the passenger door.

"It's a beautiful truck," Brian said, sliding in on the black bench seat.

Jacob climbed in and started the truck up.

"So, it's a magic truck?" Brian asked.

"I'm no 'magic truck!'" Clyde said in Jacob's head.

Jacob smiled, knowing Brian couldn't hear Clyde.

"No, he's not a 'magic truck'. He's a demon inside a Chevy C10."

"A demon?" Brian said.

"And I can hear him in my head."

Brian looked at Jacob, scowling.

"Scared the shit out of me when I first heard 'im," Jacob said.

After a second, as they pulled out of the parking lot, Brian asked "So what does Mary Lou say 'bout all this?"

"She hasn't seen Clyde yet," Jacob frowned, "She knows about the truck, but... I don't know. She's acting kinda weird lately."

"She knows 'bout how you got Clyde?" Brian asked.

"Ya, I told her."

"Maybe that's why she's acting weird. Maybe she thinks it's a fucking stupid thing to have done."

Jacob was quiet for a while, "Maybe, but I don't think so. She asked a lot of questions, but I don't know. Like I said, she's acting kinda weird. Who the fuck knows."

They drove for a time in silence.

"Ya, I might be stupid, but it's done," Jacob said.

Jacob dropped Brian off at the end of Brian's lane and drove home. In Clyde's rear-view, he could see Brian walking toward his house.

Brian was worried. When Jacob started talking about Mary Lou, graduation and his plans, Brian thought he was joking, but Jacob kept bringing it up. The whole idea of going to the crossroads and making a deal for a new truck to take Mary Lou to the prom was just dumb as fuck. Brian told him so. They laughed about it but then Jacob brought it up again. Brian started to worry Jacob was serious.

Brian told Jacob it was a stupid idea, and he was being a fucking idiot. They had words, then Jacob went quiet, which wasn't a good sign. He could be as stubborn as a bull. Afterwards, Jacob stopped talking about it.

Brian didn't see Jacob for a couple of days. He was nowhere to be found, and it felt like he was avoiding him.

This morning Brian had heard the commotion. He had known. He had known even before he was told. The school was buzzing about Jacob and his deal. "Fuck!" Brian marched around the school till he found Jacob, and shoved him, "So you just had to fucking go and do it!" Words flew, and the next thing they were outside fighting.

Now, as Brian walked to his home, he couldn't think what this would mean for his friend. Brian knew very little about The Judge and his deals. Everyone had heard of him of course, but few really wanted to talk about it, even fewer talked about their deal.

Brian hadn't told his folks about Jacob. Nor would he. It would get back to Jacob's folks, and that wouldn't be pretty. So he stewed, knowing there was nothing he could do about it.

Three days later was the Grad Dance. Brian went but didn't see Jacob or Mary Lou there. He looked around for them but assumed they blew it off and were driving around in Clyde, maybe not driving. He had had a great time. He would never admit it, but he enjoyed dancing. He rarely got a chance to. Weddings and the occasional dance at the hall, but those were few and far between. It wasn't till the next morning when he heard what had happened.

The phone rang. It was a party-line, so everyone listened to hear their code. Two longs, one short was Jacob's family ring. It rang twice before it was answered.

After a few minutes, there was a single ding indicating the phone line was free. The phone rang, one short, one long and one short. That was Brian's family ring. Brian's ma picked up the phone.

"Yes?" she said, after a pause, "Brian, it's for you." She held out the receiver. There was worry on her face.

Brian stood and took the receiver, "Yes?"

It was Jacob's dad looking for his son. There was tension in his voice.

"Naw, I didn't see him. I…" Brian said, then stopped when the phone went dead. He hung the phone up and looked at his folks, confused.

Over the next hour, the story came out. Jacob had 'accidentally' run Mary Lou over on the way to pick her up for the dance. She had died, and he was in jail waiting on an investigation.

Brian couldn't believe it. It seemed like something out of a movie. He listened to his folks talk, trying to figure out what actually happened.

Different stories were told around the town. Some were sure Jacob was guilty, maybe drinking, maybe just careless, others thought it was just a tragic accident.

After a couple of days, Jacob was released.

Brian waited for Jacob to come over, but when he didn't, he went to see him. His ma said he wasn't home. She looked worried but didn't say anything more. Brian suspected he was just upstairs, sleeping. Frustrated, he drove back home.

He found out later Jacob was spending most of his nights at the crossroads drinking, waiting for the Judge to show. He had a gun with him.

A couple months later, Brian's folks were out of town visiting his aunt, so he was having a party. Brian was surprised and happy to see Jacob walk up. He looked like hell but after a few awkward minutes it felt like old times. They sat on bails around the fire and laughed a bit. Brian started talking to a new girl, Anne. When he looked again, Jacob was gone.

The next time Brian saw Jacob was at his father's funeral. He had passed the day after the party.
Jacob was quiet, head down. Brian knew he had gone through a lot with Mary Lou's death, and now his Pa's passing. He tried to talk with him, but he was not very responsive. So Brian let him be.

It was a Tuesday in mid-August. Brian was helping his dad service machinery, getting ready for harvest. The crops were looking good, better than good. His dad was happy but watching the skies. For the last few weeks, he had hoped for rain, and it had come. Now, he needed the rain to stay away to let the crops dry out, so they could get them off before the snow came.

A couple of years ago, the rain made the fields too wet to work. They managed to swath, but they couldn't get them off the fields before the snow came. The crops stayed put over winter. The mice loved it. They multiplied like crazy. The next spring, after the frost had left and it had dried out some, Brian and his dad had picked up the swathes. Some of it was still good for feed, but much of it was ruined. Too many mice. Too much mouse shit and piss. All those mice brought on a surge of hawks, osprey and owls which Brian had loved. Raptors had always been something he was fascinated by.

Brian and his dad were prepping the baler. It was working fine, but a little time now could save hours later in the fields. A hawk sat on a post not 20 feet from Brian. He watched it as it regarded him first with one eye then the other. It was a magnificent sight.

Brian leaned in to check the spinning forming belts. It was just a slip. His runner lost its purchase on a metal surface. Just a small slip, but Brian's arms came up to stop his fall.
He didn't feel it. There was very little blood. He was suddenly lying on his back on the ground beside the bailer, and something was wrong.

From far away, he heard his dad screaming his name. He was shaking him. The hawk lifted off, all power, all grace. Brian watched it until it was out of sight.

He was in the truck, sitting in the middle, his dad holding him, his ma driving. She was driving fast. Brian was going to say something, make a joke about this truck not meant to go 70 on a gravel road, but he couldn't seem to lift his head.

Brian was standing on black sand at the edge of a slow river that moved like thick black oil. It was wide, he could just make out the other bank, and far beyond that stood what looked like silhouettes of jagged mountains. Above him were thousands of stars that reflected in the river surface and gave the black sand a shimmer. It was neither cold nor warm. There was no wind.

"This is weird," he said, "Very weird. I should go." He turned and started walking. After a while, he stopped when he realized there was no sound. He moved toward the river's edge. As he got closer, he could hear quiet lapping, it was sluggish. As he watched the river, it seemed to reach for him. He stepped back, chuckled at his foolishness and continued walking.

It was impossible to know how long he had walked when he saw something on the water in the distance. As he got closer, he could make out the shape of a large shiny black boat. It looked like one of those Viking ships he had seen in books, or a very large Venice boat. What were they called? Gondola? As he came alongside, he realized it was far more massive than he had first thought. He looked for people on board but saw no one. It seemed to be drifting with the current.

He watched it for a time, aware of the strangeness of everything around him but felt oddly calm, and unperturbed.

Behind him, he saw stone steps going up. Why hadn't I seen them before? They were huge stone steps that jutted out into the sand. He walked towards them and started climbing. The top of the stairs were lost in blackness, and after a while, the bottom was also consumed by the dark. He could no longer see the river nor the mountains, not even the stars. All there was, were these stairs. He kept climbing.

When he opened his eyes, he couldn't make sense of what he was seeing: squares, a grid of white. Everything was white. It was too bright. He squinted, trying to raise his hand to shield his eyes. He couldn't. Somehow, he couldn't raise his arm. He frowned, then he was just too tired to think about it and slipped back into sleep.

He became aware of voices. He wasn't awake, not completely, but he could hear hushed voices.

He was very thirsty. He opened his eyes when he heard his mom's voice.

"I'm thirsty," he said. He was surprised just how dry his throat was. He coughed.

His mom touched his forehead. He could see her.

"Here you go. Jus' a sip, not too much." Her voice was soft and there was a sadness in her eyes.

He sipped. It felt so good.

"What's up, Ma. Is Pa OK?" Brian asked.

"Oh, it ain't nothing. Pa's jus' fine. You don't worry. Just go to sleep. Ya need yer rest."

"Ok, Ma. I'm tired," Brian said, "My hand is cold, Ma."

As he fell back to sleep, he saw his Ma start to cry.

The next time he woke, it was dark. There was something beeping close to him. He tried to sit but couldn't seem to push himself up. He looked around the room, and was surprised to see he was in a hospital. He strained to push himself upright, grunted and failed. He looked at the ceiling for a minute. White ceiling tiles, of course, that's what they were.

His dad came into his view.

"Pa. You OK?" Brian asked.

"Ya, son. I'm jus' fine. How you feeling?"

"What's going on, Pa? Why'm I here?" Brian asked, trying and failing again to sit up.

For the first time Brian could remember, he saw his Pa's eyes fill with tears.

"There was an accident, Brian. Ya got hurt, son."

"Ah, Pa don't. Ah feel fine." Brian said, then he looked down at himself.

At first, he couldn't understand what he was seeing. It didn't make sense. He looked down, then looked into his dad's eyes then looked back at his body under the white sheet. It looked wrong. Where his right arm should have been, there was nothing, and his left arm stopped at his elbow.

"Pa? What happened? I don't understand. What's happening?"

"It's OK, son. Yer alive. We'll figure this. It's gonna be OK."

"What happened to my arms, Pa? What happened to my arms?" Brian's voice rose, edging to panic.

His Pa was pulled away, and two nurses were there holding Brian. One reached above him and did something he couldn't see. He slid down into a sleep darker and deeper than before.

The next day when he woke, Jacob was there sitting talking with his Ma. He stood when Brian opened his eyes. Brian noticed how thin Jacob had become. He looked skeletal, haggard and drawn.

"Morn," Jacob said.

Brian looked at him. Jacob's bloodshot eyes burned under his ball cap. His eyes were ringed with dark and were deeply sunk.

"Well, you look like shit," Brian said.

Jacob half grinned, "You look just as pretty as ever."

A month later when Brian got out of the hospital, it was Jacob pushing his chair at breakneck speed down the hallway and out into the sun. At that moment, it didn't feel too bad. It might be OK.

As soon as he got home, as soon as he entered where he felt safe, where everything was familiar, he knew it was never going to be OK. He knew it would never be ok again.

He couldn't touch anything. He couldn't pick up anything. Couldn't feed himself. Couldn't clean himself when he had a shit. And for how long? How long could he live with his mom feeding and wiping him up like a baby? How could he expect that of her? How could he expect that of himself?

He couldn't do it. He couldn't do any of it. He just couldn't.

"Ma, is Jacob still here?" Brian asked.

"Ya ah think Pa's still bending his ear. Did you know 'bout Jacob?"

"What 'bout Jacob?" Brian asked.

"That he's gone an' made hisself a deal wit the Judge?" His ma leaned on her hip, looking at him. "Well?"

"Ya, I knew. We got in a fight. Stopped talking for a bit. Told 'im he was a stupid fucker," Brian said.

"Watch yer language." She looked at him, "Well go talk to him now."

"K ya OK." Brian went to go outside. He stopped at the door. He couldn't open it. His ma came hurrying over and opened it for him. He didn't look at her, just walked down the steps and out in the yard.

"Hey, Bri. Yer dad was just telling me his thoughts on my life choices," Jacob grinned.

"Need ta talk to you, Jacob," Brian said, looking at his dad. His dad took the hint.

"Nice talking with ya, Jacob. Thanks for yer help with Brian here," he said.

"No problem," Jacob said as Brian's dad walked away. "What's up, Bri?"

"Ah can't do this," Brian said.

Jacob didn't respond.

"Ah just can't do it. None of it. Ah can't have my Ma feedin' me, wiping my ass."

"And?"

"An' I want you to help me."

"Well, I ain't wipin' yer ass," Jacob said smiling.

"You know what ah mean. Ah need to see him. Ah need to see him tonight." Brian said.

"Ya sure, you don't wanna think about it for a couple of days?"

"Fuck no. I'm not waiting."

"No deal goes the way ya think."

"I fucking don't care. I want my arms back."

"Alright. I'll come get ya later."

"Nope. I'm coming with ya now. Ma and Pa are goin' to try to talk me owda it. I'm not goin' to let 'em." Brian said.

Jacob shrugged, "Ok, let's get goin'."

They walked over to Clyde. Jacob opened the door and boosted Brian in. They drove down the driveway. Jacob saw Brian's Ma come out onto the porch in the rearview.

They drove around most of the day, checking fields and talking. They talked about everything other than what Brian was planning to do. They talked about girls, about trucks and farming. They retold stories about shit they did. They told each other lies, each knowing the lie, each laughing nonetheless. Around a quarter to midnight, they pulled up to the crossroads. Jacob put Clyde into 'Park.'

"Ok, what are you going to ask for?" Jacob asked.

"I'm gonna ask for my arms back."

"Ya sure?"

"Well, that's what I want."

"Ah bin thinkin'. I was wondering if ya maybe wanted to ask for something that protects you from this sort of thing happening again," Jacob said.

Brian looked at Jacob.

"Yer sellin' yer soul. Might as well get more than just yer arms. If yer gonna do it, do it big."

"Like you?" Brian said.

Jacob scowled, "Ya well do as I say not as I fuckin' did."

Jacob checked his watch. He got out of the truck, walked around and opened the door. He helped Brian down from Clyde.

"Don't think the Judge'll show if I'm here. This is sumthin' yer gonna have to do on yer own." Jacob said.

He climbed into Clyde. "I'll come back for ya in an hour. Good luck." Jacob drove off.

Brian stood in the middle of the crossroads and waited. The air was cool. He looked around. He could see Clyde's taillights fading into the distance. Far off to the south, a yard light marked a farmyard. Probably Peterson's place.

He looked up at the dark sky. It was filled with stars; they reminded him of the stars that glinted off that black river.

Suddenly he was surrounded by bright inescapable light. A car roared to a stop inches from Brian's legs. After a second, the engine shut down, and the lights went out. As his eyes adjusted, he saw a tall man in a fine suit stepping towards him. "Brian, my boy, what can I do you for?"

An hour later, Jacob drove back to the crossroads. Brian was standing there tall and whole, naked from the waist up. Jacob got out of the truck and walked to him.

"Well? It looks like it worked out," Jacob said.

Brian flexed. He had a huge grin on his face.

"I feel great!" he said and stretched out his arms as wide as he could, relishing the feel of them.

"Humm, Brian's changed, more than him having arms again. There's something else here," Clyde said in Jacob's head.

"So… what did you make your deal for?"

Brian grinned, "I am invincible!"

"Ok, but what's your deal?"

"That's it. Anything that hurts me makes me stronger."

"That's it? Ya sure? The Judge always has a twist." Jacob was skeptical.

"Nope, that's it. Said sumptin' about balance, but I was watching my arms grow, jus' like that. It hurt something fierce, but it was so cool to watch 'em. Kinda missed what he was talking about, and…oh ya, that fucking creepy dude! Mr. November. What the fuck is that? Just grinning like an idiot, talkin' 'bout contracts and waiving clauses an' some shit. I DON'T KNOW! Just some shit."

"That 'shit' is the important part. Fuck, Brian! Now we don't know what's going to happen. Ya got two new arms. It ain't gonna be fer free. Believe me, it ain't gonna be so easy."
Brian stomped his foot like a child denied ice cream.

"Well, fuck! I don't know, do I?" Brian said, "Co'mon, let's git back to da farm. Ma is going to be freakin', and ah gotta explain. Now that's not gonna be pretty!"

Jacob agreed, and they walked back to Clyde.

"What are you gonna tell yer folks?" Jacob asked.

"I donno. Not much a kin say 'ceptin I met with The

Judge. New arms is a bit hard ta hide." Brian said with a wry smile.

They drove the half-hour back to Brian's farm in silence, each lost in their own thoughts.

"Drop me off here. It's late. I don't wanna wake them with yer roaring around the yard," Brian said.

Jacob hadn't been planning any 'roaring around', but he didn't say anything, just slowed Clyde and pulled to a stop on the gravel road at the end of Brian's lane.

"Nite, Jacob," Brian said, "Talk to you in the morn if I'm still around." Brian grinned, flexed his new arms, and slid out of the truck.

Jacob waited for Brian to start walking, and with a wave, turned Clyde around and headed home.

"His deal seems pretty standard. I don't feel a lot of threads around it," Clyde said.

"Threads?" Jacob asked.

"Ya, every contract has its 'clauses.' They show like threads, thin coloured lines wrapped around the soul stretching to the other plane. They are what tie the soul to the devil."

"And mine?" Jacob asked.

"Yours is simple, but his has two threads I don't understand. I don't think I have ever seen these. I really don't know what they mean," Clyde answered as they turned into Jacob's lane and drove up to the house.

The house was dark, only the yardlight casting its solid shadows. One shadow stood and walked up to greet Jacob and Clyde.

"Hey, Doc," he said, but he did not reach out to pet the massive German Shepherd. He knew better. He walked to the house and closed the screen door quietly. His mom would have woken when he drove into the yard, but there was no need to further disturb her with the screen door bang.

Early the next morning, Brian was banging on Jacob's door. Jacob's Ma was up doing her morning baking. You'd have to show up pretty damn early to catch her in bed.

"C'mon in," she called from the kitchen.

Brian walked in. The screen door gave a plaintive cry and banged shut, ensuring Jacob would be up or at least aware that Brian had arrived.

"Wacha bakin'?" Brian asked, peering over her shoulder.

"Just some fresh bread. It ain't ready. Nother 10 minutes. Go git Jacob and I'll fix ya some brea…" She stopped, shock on her face that turned to horror as she realized what she was seeing.

"YOU DUMB FUCK!" She nearly screamed, "YOU went to see the Judge!"

Brian stepped back just as Jacob stumbled into the kitchen. Brian had never heard Jacob's Ma raise her voice in anger, let alone swear.

"What's all the ruckus?" Jacob said.

"An' ah suppose you put 'im up to it?" She turned on Jacob.

"Hell no. I tried ta talk 'im out of it." Jacob raised his hands as he backed up.

She glared at the two cowering boys, each several heads taller than her. After a time, she shook her head. There was a resigned sadness in her eyes.

"Well, youz might as well have some breakfast," she said.

Brian looked to Jacob, shrugged and sat. Jacob pulled his t-shirt on, and sat across from Brian.

"I can't imagine yer Ma's none too happy."

"No shit," Brian said, "That's why I'm here. Bin yelled at since two this morn. When Pa's voice got hoarse, Ma set in. Never did git a word in edgewise." He gave Jacob a grin.

Ma saw and scowled, holding two plates of bacon and eggs with toast.

"Yer Ma haz every right to yell atcha. I thought you were just a mite smarter than my fool child, here." She looked at Jacob.

Brian looked down at his plate as Ma put it down in front of him.

"Well, seems to me there's plenty of work round here for two strong young men with too much energy," Ma said.

"Yes, ma,am," Jacob said, digging into his breakfast, "the old barn's nearly fallin' in on itself. Thought maybe we'd pull er down."

"Ya don't think it's dry enough to finish the south quarter?" Ma asked.

"After breakfast, we'll drive over and check, but ah don't think so. Not much sand in that there ground." Jacob said around a mouthful of egg.

Sunday morning, Brian's mom called from the kitchen, "Brian?" She waited, "Brian? We're heading ta church. Maybe you wanna come?" She waited, "Brian? Ya, hear me, boy?"

"Leave it be, Ma. I ain't gonna be goin' ta no church an' you know it." Brian called down from his room.

His Ma looked at Pa and shook her head, shrugged and pushed Pa out the kitchen door.

Brian went back to sleep.

The church Brian's folks went to was just over a half an hour away in the tiny village of Accord. They turned right out of their drive, headed west on 78, turned north on 89 across 11 and 10 minutes further. On a Sunday, the village was quiet, with no vehicles except for churchgoers.

The church was built in the 40's. It was a small, white-painted wood building, pretty and well kept. It had a tiny steeple. Its bell rang out as Brian's folks pulled up and parked.

Service was an hour. The minister rambled on about being vigilant about the devil. It seemed to be directed at them personally as if the minister knew what Brian had done.

Afterward, Brian's folks shook hands with the minister and walked down the steps.

They looked at each other when they got into their car. A plan, they needed a plan to save their son. They sat talking quietly. Trying to figure out if now was the time to talk with the minister, maybe get his help. He was very young, very inexperienced, and he was new to Accord. He still didn't know much about the Judge and his hold on the area. He would be of little use. They would need to find another way.

That decided, they drove out of the parking lot and headed home, south on 89 out of the village and stopped at highway 11. It was just past noon on a bright, beautiful Sunday. Pa checked west, checked east, then he pulled out. Ma was feeling hopeful they could find a way to save their son now they had decided to. She opened her mouth to comment on the day.

Stanley Robertson was in his early 70s, still sharp as a

tack, but his eyes were going, and the beer between his legs wasn't his first. When Brian's Pa pulled out in front of him, he reacted as best as he could. Stanley was driving his old Massey Ferguson truck loaded with some 80 bales of hay. He yanked the truck hard to the right, too late. His truck began to roll over, spilling the bales of hay over the pavement, and clipped the back of Brian's folks' car, sending it into a spin.

The car spun in a broad, almost slow arch into the path of an eastbound semi. The tractor-trailer with its glittering tank on the back, rammed into them from behind. It was speeding.

The much heavier semi shoved the car forward. The front of the car was flung upward into the air. At this point, Brian's folks were still alive and were shoved violently into their seats. The car rolled upside down over the truck's massive tank of gas. It ignited. The explosion was felt several miles away, the sound carried much farther. The fire lasted for hours and melted the pavement below the tangled metal. It looked like a scene from hell.

If Brian had been awake and in the yard, he might have been able to hear the accident. He would have definitely been able to see the cloud of black smoke that roiled into the sky.
 yard, he might have been able to hear the accident. He would have definitely been able to see the cloud of black smoke that roiled into the sky.

# CHAPTER 5

## THE REFUSAL

### "TEEN'S DEATH DEEMED ODD"

The heading in the newspaper was short. It went on to describe the accident.

Teri Sue Anderson was struck and killed by a northbound motorist in the early morning on March 22nd at the crossroads of 89 and 78. Constable M. Miller, in a press conference held early this morning, said, "It appears Miss Anderson had been performing a sort of ritual." He did not elaborate on the accident, saying there was an 'ongoing investigation.' Memorial services will be held at Franklin's funeral home on Thursday.

Seven days later, under a moonless sky, Teri crawled from the grass and weeds at the side of the road just beside the stop sign on 78. She was naked, cold and bruised. She was also bewildered and alive.

She looked around; her clothes were gone. As she stood in the middle of the crossroads, she could not remember what had happened or how she'd ended up in the ditch.

Teri had been preparing for that night for weeks. This had been something she had thought about and wanted to do for over a year. The idea had come from a book she had found by accident. The book had a spell that would bring the power of Gaia if she read it correctly. She had researched further, reading everything she could find in the school library, which wasn't much.

Her mom had been happy to see her spending so much time reading and not just the horror books she usually favoured. She wouldn't have been happy had she known what Teri was planning...even though her favourite show was Bewitched.

Over the last year, Teri had started to pull away from her mom, and from many of her friends. She wanted to hide. She knew she was considered weird by most of the popular girls with their teased-up hair and pastel angora sweaters. She had dark hair that she left long, and dressed in an oversized sweater she stole from her dad. They called her a beatnik, with a dismissive sneer. She wasn't sure why they would call her that. She wasn't into poetry or coffee. Maybe there were other definitions to it.

She wanted to be on her own. To be allowed to live life as she wanted, not shoved into the role that everyone expected of her. Secretary, nurse or mother seemed to be the only ones her father thought she would be suitable for. That was not her. She wanted so much more. She hated the assumptions, hated the expectations that she was just a girl who would become a woman who would fulfill the role given to her.

The book described a power from the earth that would give her the strength she felt she needed, a power she could use to remove herself from the world.

If she was honest with herself, she had everything prepared for the enchantment for almost two weeks. She had done all the research she could. She had read and reread the passages she needed. She had to admit she was afraid. She told herself it was all going to be good, that one night would give her all she wanted, but doubt crept in. What if it didn't work and she would have to return to the world she hated without this single hope?

In spite of her terror, she had ridden her bike to the crossroads. She carried very little, just what she needed.

She moved quickly, not wanting to have a moment to think, to doubt and stop. Looking up and down the road, making sure no one was going to see her nakedness, she took her clothes off and folded them neatly at the side of the road.

She kneeled down in front of the open book. The pavement was cold and bit into her bare knees. She started but stumbled almost right away. She knew she had to complete the entire incantation in one go. She had memorized it but still had it in front of her. It wasn't particularly long or complex, but she was nervous.

She started again. She was nearly halfway through when there was an explosion of light, and then she could remember nothing. It just went black.

She hugged herself against the night air chill as goosebumps raced across her body.

The roar of the engine and the blast of light made her jump in fright.

She stood pale in the headlights, trying to cover herself. Her eyes wide, the whites shining like a trapped animal.

The car that stood mere feet from her roared once more before quieting. The night sounds, by comparison, were very quiet. The doors opened, two tall silhouettes rose out of the car and walked slowly toward her. She backed up a step.

"Oh, not to worry, Teri. Mr. June, please give Teri here something to cover herself," said the driver. He was a tall, handsome man in a fine dark suit and a sparkling smile.

The passenger was even taller, very thin. He, too, was smiling, but it had a manic feel with no warmth. He wore a broad-brimmed black hat.

He stepped forward, smiling, and slid off his suit jacket and reluctantly handed it to her.

Tentatively she stretched out her hand, grabbed the jacket and turned her back. She pulled it on. It felt cold and slightly scratchy against her skin.

"So, Teri. How are you feeling this fine evening?"

"I...I... Who are you?" Teri asked. She clutched the jacket closed with her hands tight to her neck.

"Oh, I am sorry. I assumed you knew since you called. Around here, they call me The Judge."

"The Judge! You're not the Judge," she said.

"Am I not?"

"No. You are not him! You are not." She paused, "You can't be."

The Judge smiled, "Not what you were expecting?"

She looked at him, her head down slightly, "No."

"What were you hoping for?" he said, smiling. His teeth glinted.

"Well ...Not you," she said.

He laughed and looked to Mr. June, who looked back and smiled. The Judge scowled.

He turned back to Teri and smiled. "Well, I assure you I am he."

Teri looked at him. She looked at him askew.

"Come on, Teri, what can I do for you?"

"I want the power." She stepped forward, her head held high and thrust forward, an image of a woman of power.

"The power?" he smiled, "Well, of course, you do."

His smile suddenly vanished, leaving a cruel, hard face. He examined her closely. His eyes went glossy and black like the eyes of a shark. He leaned forward, looking down on her. She stood her ground for as long as she could, then she faltered and stepped back.

He straightened, and the whites of his eyes returned with his white-toothed smile.

"Well. That was impressive. Most of you wilt far quicker. You will be powerful. You will serve me very well."

"Serve you?"

"Yes, of course. Where do you think the power comes from?"

"From the earth! From Gaia! The mother goddess!" she cried. Her voice rose as tears rolled down her cheeks. Suddenly she was a girl, again. "The goddess." Her voice was small and quiet.

His smile grew. Now it had real pleasure. It was a most terrible smile.

"This is SO sweet," he glanced at Mr. June briefly, scowled, then back to Teri. He watched her, his terrible smile never leaving his face.

She looked down, beaten.

"So sweet," he said. "Ok. Mr. June, is the paperwork in order?"

"Yes, sir. All in order," Mr. June smiled.

"I dismiss you," the Judge said.

Mr. June's smile faded slightly. He disintegrated, crumpling into a cloud of dying black flies. The coat wrapped around Teri broke apart into a shimmering mass of flies sloughing off her body. She screamed, jumping back, her hands flapping in disgust.

She stopped, her body jerked, then stiffened. She stood upright, her head back, mouth open. Her eyes, all white. Her arms spread out wide.

She was thrown violently to the ground. She landed hard with a bone-deep thud. Her body was twisted, rotating on her back, scraping against the pavement until each of her limbs pointed down one of the roads that made up the crossroads.

She lay there, spread-eagled. The Judge watched her. He watched the power enter her. The power smashed into her through her mouth, her nose, her ears, through every orifice. It exploded out of her eyes and her fingertips. It swirled around, lashing at her naked pale body. Her body jerked. It spasmed, thrashing around under the onslaught. Her eyes burned, flared bright and darkened like cooling molten metal till they were completely black.

Smiling, the Judge turned and climbed into his shiny black car and drove into the dark.

Teri lay on the cold pavement, staring up at the stars that reflected in her shiny black eyes.

A slight colouring to the east was just showing when Teri stood. She moved in small bird-like motions, seemingly confused and unfamiliar with her body. A foreign machine never manipulated before. In a way, that was true. She now shared her physical presence with a creature, newly born, not quite an entity on its own, not aware of itself, a bundle of instinct and power, immense power. It wrapped itself around the being that was Teri. It intertwined itself, knitting itself into her until the separation blurred, until the boundaries that defined Teri shifted, and she became more.

She became a power.

She stood, looked around and started to walk.

The sun was barely peeking over the horizon. Her naked form stood out starkly white against the shifting yellows and oranges of the imminent sunrise. A patrol car's headlights lit her up. Its cherry top came on, washing her skin in pulsing scarlet.

The young cop stepped from his car, talking rapidly on his mic. He tossed the mic down on the seat and started towards the girl. She had not noticed him.

"Miss? Can I help you? Are you OK?" His voice was shaky, uncertain. His Adam's apple bounced.

He stepped in front of her. She stopped walking, stood, arms by her sides, looking through him.

"Miss?" he said.

Her black marble eyes refocused and saw him. She reached forward with her left hand, raising it slowly toward his cheek. He watched her, watched her hand, unsure of what to do.

His training did not include this sort of situation.

Her left index finger came up and touched him. A spark, like static electricity arced from his cheek. Another, this time larger and more violent, flashed bluish white. It lit up his face. He pulled back, startled.

She grasped his shoulder with her right hand, a hungry desperation giving her strength. She pressed her left palm to his cheek. Sparks swirled around them, fine lines of blue flared blinding white just as the sun crested the horizon.

The flash faded, replaced by the golden light of the morning sun. The cobalt blue shadows that fingered across the road striped a bizarre scene.

Two bodies lay at opposite sides of the road as if blown apart by an explosion. The young cop lay with his arm and face partially in the grass and weeds.

The woman on her back, pale as porcelain, floated six inches off the pavement. Around her head, her hair drifted languidly, as if underwater. Her eyes were open. The black glossiness slowly faded till they were white. As her eyes began to close, the white faded to reveal the pretty brown that had belonged to Teri Sue Anderson.

When the second patrol car arrived, Teri was lying on the pavement breathing shallowly; however, the young cop on the side of the road was not.

An ambulance was called, and with the ambulance came more cops, followed soon after by the Chief. He came to see, 'just what the fuck was going on' as he had said.

The strip of the road soon filled with cars, reflectors and cones, reducing it to a single lane. The Chief strode up to the scene, in command and determined to find answers. He had lost a young officer, and that was unacceptable. He looked into the ambulance at the prone girl.

"Well, is she fucking dead, or is she alive?" he called out to anyone who might be able to give him an answer.

Everyone scurried about trying to look like they knew what they were doing because no one really knew what was going on.

Teri was lying in the ambulance, ready to be rushed to the hospital just as soon as the Chief said it was OK.

After a lot of head-scratching, Teri was taken to the hospital. The young officer was taken to the morgue.

The heading in the news was somewhat confused and even shorter than before. "Teri Sue Anderson's death even odder. She's NOT dead."

To say the investigation was confused would be an understatement. There were so many questions and no answers.

When the detective assigned to the challenging task went to the morgue to see Teri's body, he found the shiny cold metal drawer empty. The morgue tech had no idea how. He had put her in it. He remembered. He had the paperwork.

They had been overloaded, so they hadn't had a chance to get to her scheduled autopsy. It had been pushed to Monday, but she was found alive, making the autopsy somewhat unnecessary.

The detective was trying, but without a dead body, he wasn't investigating a death. He was investigating...what? As far as he was concerned, it was just a mistake. Just a fuck up in the paperwork. When he filed his report, it was thin, and he knew it. It was accepted without comment. Everyone was embarrassed that somehow a young girl was listed as dead, then suddenly alive.

The police called Teri's parents for the second time in a week. The first call had destroyed their world. The second turned it upside down.

It was her father, Jack, who picked up the phone. He listened, not sure what the officer was saying. He looked to his wife, Alice, confused.

She couldn't understand the look on her husband's face.

She rose and took the phone from his hand and listened to the officer explain that Teri had been found alive.

Alice didn't know what to say. The officer repeated his message when he got no response. After a minute, he told them she is in the hospital and that they should come down and see her.

Somehow, that got through. They left immediately, still unsure what they would find when they got to the hospital.

When they walked through the sliding doors into the hospital, they stood looking around in a daze. Every nurse, every doctor knew who they were, knew about the not dead girl.

Teri's parents were directed to their daughter's room. Alice broke down when she saw Teri lying in the hospital bed, nearly as white as the sheets but alive. Crying, Alice ran into the room. She sat and held Teri's hand. From that point on, she didn't leave Teri's side.

Teri remained asleep for seven days, her eyes darting back and forth violently under her lids as if she were watching something terrible or reading something horrible.

Doctors came and went. Each offered their reassurances, each time becoming less reassuring. They ran tests and more. The tests they completed were inconclusive, always inconclusive. All they could say is that she was healthy with no reason for her to be in a coma.

Then one afternoon, she woke. Her mom was sitting by

her when Teri opened her eyes. The first thing she saw was the square tiled ceiling. It confused her. It didn't make sense.

Beside her, her mother yelped in surprise and excitement.

Teri looked toward her. She didn't know who this woman was, just a woman crying for no reason. Then a name filtered into Teri's mind.

"Alice. This is Alice," she thought, and for some reason, that made her smile, and the woman named Alice exploded into more tears and started yelling.

The small room was very quickly filled with people touching, talking and crying. Teri watched it all, bewildered.

Her parents were so happy. They had their daughter back after spending a week believing she was dead, then another week watching her sleep, not knowing if she would ever wake up.

They thanked the doctors, Jack shaking everyone's hands. The doctors smiled, still completely baffled but happy to have the problem solved and the mystery out of their hands.

Her parents took Teri home, happy to have their daughter home safe and alive. Teri sat in the back seat of the car, looking around. She knew these smiling people, knew their names, knew who they were to her, but somewhere she couldn't feel it. She could not touch the part of her that loved them. She was sure she loved them. They were her parents, so she must love them.

Her mother, Alice, leaned over the back of the seat and talked nonstop. She kept reaching back to touch Teri, as if to make sure she was real.

Teri watched her mother. For all her happiness of having Teri back, there was something under the surface, a tension around her eyes, a tightness that Teri didn't understand. Teri thought back to what she could remember of her mom before.

She knew things hadn't been great. She thought back over the last few weeks. They had fought. Teri had said things she wished she could take back. Even now, as disconnected as she was, she knew she had been cruel.

Her dad, Jack, was quiet, maybe quieter than usual. He just drove, occasionally glancing in the mirror at Teri. She couldn't read him. She hadn't been close to him. He was a presence in her life, of course. He was cold, distant, a solid man-shaped object that moved through the edges of her life.

They pulled into the yard. Her dad shut off the car. He sat for a minute holding the steering wheel in both hands, then got out and walked to the garage without saying a word.

Alice continued chatting, not noticing. She never noticed. She led Teri to the house, smiling and talking.
Teri felt a stirring of a feeling she recognized. It was distant, buried deep, but it was strong. It was something she had felt for a long time. It was somewhere between anger and disgust. She wasn't sure where to point it, but it was there.

Teri and her mom walked through the house, Teri recognizing everything, all the while feeling disconnected from it all.

Teri went upstairs to her room. She looked around. She could find no connection to it. It felt like it belonged to someone else, someone she knew very well. Someone she had spent a lot of time with. Someone she was close to, but not her.

The photos scattered about of her friends and her laughing. She remembered the moments, but they were like scenes from a movie she had watched a long time ago. The young, naive girl that had lived in this room, who had read and dreamed of her life, was gone. Teri was no longer that child.

Her mom hovered in the doorway behind her, her anxiety and tension radiating off her in waves. After weeks of unbelievable pain, after being told her daughter was dead, then that she was, in fact, not dead, left her in a state of confusion, not sure how to proceed. Not really knowing what was real.

Teri turned to her mom and smiled weakly, "I'm tired."

"Of course, dear, of course. We'll leave you be. Dinner at six?" Her mother asked.

"Hmm... Ya. Sure."

"We're just so happy to have you home safe," her mom said. She hugged Teri, then started to cry as she turned and left the room, closing the door behind her.

Teri looked at the closed door. She knew she should be sad for her mom, knew that it was her fault they were so sad, but she couldn't feel it. Not really.

Teri turned and regarded her room. She went and sat on her bed. She considered her bookcase with her books and treasures.

There was something else different, something she couldn't put her finger on. She looked at the books, each one she had read and loved, but one stood out. It was an old black book with a torn spine and faded gold letters.

She had bought it recently in a junk store in the city when she and her mom had gone to town on some errand. They had been walking along when Teri had glanced into the shop window and saw a stack of old books. One of the books seemed to call to her. She couldn't have explained how, but there was something.

She had left her mom to run her errand and went in to buy the book.

The spine of the book read "Spells and Incantations for the Modern Wicca." She slid it out from under another book. It was old and nearly falling apart. The pages were very brown, with a dry, brittle feel, and many were loose, but it was perfect.

It cost all her babysitting money. When she showed it to her mom, she got a heavy sigh and an eye roll, but it didn't diminish the excitement.

In her room, she rose from the bed and took a step forward, looking at the book. What was it? It was just a black spine, but it stood out.

Suddenly she realized why. She looked around the room; the comprehension sweeping over her.

There was almost no colour in anything. Everything was almost black and white. She looked back at the book. It was a black-covered book, but it had colour. She pulled it from the shelf.

This is where she found the incantation to draw power from the goddess. She now knew it had been a lie. It was just a trap to draw naïve people to the Judge and make them his servants.

"Oh..." she said as the memory of the young cop's surprised face came to her. The young cop she took from. He hadn't been much older than she was.

She had killed him, that was clear, not shadowed at all. She had felt him as she took from him. She had felt everything he was, had been. She had felt him enter her. She had taken his everything. She felt the horror as she remembered feeling his terror, his confusion as he slipped away. She cried. She could, would, never do that again.

She would never let herself be that monster that had taken. Never again. She would never be a tool for the Judge.
She felt anger grow in her, a nugget of molten heat. She felt her fingers tingle with the anger, and she felt something else. The book: not only was it in colour in a mostly black and white world, but it was also warm.

"No," she thought, "Not warm. Something else." She

held the book in two hands, and as she did, the 'warmth' spread from it to her hands, up her wrists, up her arms till it reached her chest. A soft moan came from her lips as the warmth that was not warmth spread through her.

Colour came back into the world. Not full vibrant colour, but some colour. She looked around the room and smiled at the colour in all things.

She realized she was no longer tired. Just seconds ago, she was ready to lay down and sleep. Now she was wide awake, as if she had just woken from a good night's sleep.

She walked over to her desk, sat and opened the book. In many ways, it was a book of recipes, not for cooking but for preparing to cast small incantations that were mostly just stylized prayers. When she had first brought the book home, she had been disappointed. She had started reading the pages and found nothing in the book that looked like it was what she was hoping for.

She had wanted it to give her power, so she would not feel so powerless. She was tired of being ignored at school. She was so tired of feeling that she didn't matter, that she was just another angry teen, another suicide waiting to happen.

She had nearly thrown the book out after reading a few pages, looking for answers and finding only wandering, vague text talking about the love of the goddess and earth. It was so frustrating.

But she didn't and then found the incantation that seemed to say it would bring power. She read the incantation and reread it. It did seem to have a call, an actual call to bring on power. Then she had the idea to do the chant at the crossroads. She knew that there was power there.

She wasn't going there to call the Judge. She was going to call his opposite.

She had watched a late-night horror movie about witches, and they always seemed to do their magic in the nude, so she would too. That seemed appropriate. Bare yourself to the goddess to receive her blessing, her power.

Now, as she sat at her desk holding the book, feeling that warmth sliding into her, she, with the power in her, opened the pages with a different eye.

Much of the book was just as she thought, worthless. Just some writer's fantasy but sprinkled in amongst the pages were little pieces of real wisdom, real magic. She was flipping pages enjoying the swirl of tiny vortexes of colour as though each page, each letter was covered with tiny, coloured dust.

She turned a page, and the next page burst with colour. It spilled out and swirled around the book and her fingers. Each letter danced with a vibrant colour that faded as she read the words. They stood out with colour around them. These she read carefully, and as she did, they faded from the book.

She panicked as she watched the beautiful colours fade, leaving the age-stained paper blank and diminished.

She stopped reading and looked back at the blank pages. The words were still there as barely legible faded marks, but as she stared at the marks, she smiled as the words returned, not as colourful as when she first read them. They did come back and then faded again as soon as she looked away from them.

Cautiously at first, she continued reading. She lost time to the book until she heard her mother call from downstairs that supper was ready. Teri looked up, surprised. It was dark outside. She had read the day away.

She closed the book and laid both hands on top of the tired cover. She closed her eyes and felt the words inside the book. She could see them in her mind, read them, the colours whirling inside her mind. She pulled them from the book into herself. All the words she hadn't yet read flooded into her mind, filling it. She felt that strange warmth filled her. She felt electrified. She vibrated with power that she did not recognize but somehow did.

She walked downstairs filled with power. She imagined herself surrounded with warmth and colour.

"Well, you look better," Teri's mom said as she looked up. There was real surprise on her face. She looked at Teri, then to Teri's father, then back, "Are you hungry, dear?"

Teri thought for a minute, then realized that she was, "Yes, actually I am," she replied.

Teri sat at the table at her spot without thinking. Her dad pulled out his chair and sat, watching Teri warily.

"I made your favourite." Teri's mom said. The pride rested uneasily on her face.

Teri couldn't remember what that could be. She smiled, waiting to be told.

"My famous Mac and cheese."

"Ah, yes. That's great." Teri said as her mom put a large casserole dish down on the wooden table. She didn't say anything. Teri's father looked less than happy. He sat in his chair with a sour look on his face.

Teri smiled, unsure what to say. She vaguely remembered thinking this had been her favourite when she was little, maybe six, but she was sure it hadn't been recently.

She smiled at her mom, "Great."

Her mom leaned in and gave a sideways hug, tears filling her eyes. Teri reached up and touched her mom's arm. A spark leapt from her arm to Teri's finger.

Teri's mom yelped and pulled away, rubbing her arm. Teri felt the jolt run up her arm. She felt the power, power that she pulled from her mom.

Her mom sat heavily, mumbling about static electricity.

They ate in silence. As soon as she was finished, Teri stood, took her plate to the sink and said, "I'm still feeling very tired..."

"Of course, sweetie. I feel pretty tired, as well. It's been a difficult week. You go to bed and get a good night's sleep. I think I'll leave the dishes till tomorrow," Teri's mom said, looking at the dishes. She shrugged and went to stand. She sat back down, "Oh...I musta stood up too fast."

Teri looked at her, worried.

"Oh, I'm ok," Alice stood, brushing her apron with both hands, "I'm just fine. Just a bit dizzy. You go to bed, sweetie." She leaned forward and kissed Teri on the cheek. Teri braced slightly, expecting a shock that didn't happen.

"K, nite, mom. Nite, dad," Teri said as she went up to her room. She heard her father grunt.

Her room was full of colour. It had been so hard to pretend to be tired. She felt so full, full of colour and energy, so full she was nearly vibrating.

She looked around the room. Each object had multiple colours, like rainbows radiating outward. Some pulsed, some shimmered like heat haze. Each was distinct and separate while being part of a whole. She moved around the room, her fingers lightly touching each object, feeling the different feel of each, feeling the various vibrations each individual object gave off.

Some were just passive objects that sat quietly while others seemed to hold more, seemed to almost want to talk, to tell their story, their reason for existence and their place. At these she paused, lingering to allow their stories to unfold. She moved on as the next object called out to her until she circled her room and arrived at her bookcase.

The books held the brightest colours. Slowly she touched

each book in turn, and each book told its truth. Many held very little, only a shadow of a story. Others held more. More story, more truth, but none shone as bright as the book she had found at the junk store in town.

She smiled. She knew its truths.

She turned from the bookcase, and her eyes caught the small succulent her best friend Kiley had given her. It pulsed differently than the things in her room. There were little threads of sparkling coloured light leading off into the air.

She reached forward and touched its rough green surface. Instantly the coloured threads curled and spiralled around her wrist and in her arm. A warmth slid into her fingers. She felt it flowing into her. It felt amazing

Her head folded back as her eyes closed. She could taste the life, green and moist. It burst in her mind, in her mouth, in her body, then the texture changed.

It darkened, to a soot texture, an ashy taste.

Her head came forward, and her eyes popped open. She looked at the tiny succulent. It was brown with blackened edges. It was dead.

She felt the death, tasted the dark. She pulled her hand back slowly, staring at the plant she had killed.

She thought of her mother and the spark that had passed between them. She could still feel the texture of the power she took from her mother. She recognized it now that she knew what it was. She understood its nuance. The power was what made her mother. She could feel her fear, her sadness, her anger, frustration and her hopes.

Teri knew her mom all her life but never the whole of her. The complete human that was her mother. Now she realized she did. That small spark opened Teri's mom like a book to Teri. She loved her more than she ever had before.

Now she knew teenager Alice's pain and isolation. Teri felt every heartbreak, every triumph, every kindness, every cruelty. She heard her every happiness and her every sadness.

As she let her mother's life, Alice's life, wash over her, she suddenly knew older Alice's loss. There had been a baby before Teri, before Jack. A baby lost, given away. A mistake. Teri cried. She sat and felt her mother.

She wasn't sure how long she sat on the edge of her bed. It was dark out when she looked up.

She stood and listened to the quiet house. Her parents were asleep. The house was asleep.

She walked slowly down the steps and stood in the kitchen. Here some objects called to her. Some spoke to her in her mother's voice, an inner voice Teri now recognized.

She walked from the house out across the porch and stepped on the grass. She was barefooted, and her body electrified as the green life flooded up her legs.

At first, it was unbelievable. It rushed up her body, power flowing through her limbs. Pulsating out down her arms to her fingers, then returning, but then it became too much, and it overwhelmed her.

She struggled to return to the steps, she was falling. She fell backwards, landing on her back. She was wearing jeans and a t-shirt. Where her bare skin touched the grass, the power started moving into her. It burned her. She writhed on the ground.

She felt the grass, felt its massive life, felt further down, she could feel the thousands of small living creatures that teemed in and below the grass, and then she went still.

She felt something else. Below the grass and weeds, below the insects, bugs and worms, was something else, something larger. As she opened herself to it, she realized what it was, and the power there terrified her.

It was the earth. It was the one, the power she had originally sought. She felt its massive weight. She had only glimpsed the smallest fraction of it.

It was the beginning and the ending. It was the source. She knew this power here. It was the same as she carried, only what she had in her was only the smallest fragment, the tiniest sliver. It was far beyond her. If she touched it, it would consume her.

She could feel the power was not for her, not for any mortal being to touch directly. Inside her, she felt the power sing to the power below her. If she touched that power, what made her her would cease to be. She would become part of the world power, no longer Teri.

She shrank from it. Gasping, she sucked in the night air then breathed out. As her breath touched the night air, she understood the warmth was tied to her breath. She found she had control of the flow of her power. She didn't have to suck from everything that she touched. She could stop the flow, even reverse it.

She pulled back from the power that was so immense, pulled back from the myriad of tiny powers, pulled back from the grass and breathed.

Slowly she stood. She could feel the power beneath her, but it no longer flowed into her. It was just there.

She felt alive, like she had never felt. She walked on the grass, listening to its story.

Her fingertips brushed a small bush, and its story sang to her.

She walked to a line of trees that marked the edge of her

family's home. Her fingers reached out, and she rejoiced in the tree's songs.

She stood there, her fingers touching the leaves until morning rose and spread warmth across the lawn, and she felt the song of the trees, of the grass, change to welcome the sun and its life-giving warmth.

When she returned to the house, her mother was up sitting at the kitchen table, drinking a coffee in her robe. She looked tired, with dark circles under her eyes. She looked up at Teri and smiled.

"Good morning, Teri. Just give me a minute, and I'll make you some breakfast," she said.

"Oh, no rush. I'm fine," Teri said. She walked behind her mom, her fingers lightly touched her mother's shoulders, and she returned the energy that she had stolen the night before. She returned it plus a little of what she had taken from the grass outside.

Immediately her mother straightened in her chair, and the dark circles faded. The light in her eyes brightened. The tired weight lifted from her, "See, all I needed was a sit-down and a coffee."

Teri smiled as her father came in looking for a coffee.

"You both are looking better." Jack grunted, "coffee?"

She knew the day her mother was going to die. The knowing came to her one morning as she had finished helping her mom bake fresh bread. She had hugged her mom as she went out for her morning walk.

She felt it in the air. Saw it in the way the sunlight bounced off the curl of a tree leaf. She knew its coming days before, in the texture of the snow on her early morning walk and the arch of a swallow's flight. She sensed it in the taste of her morning tea and the way dew dripped off blades of grass.

She tried giving her mother life, pushing forward into her through light touches on the shoulders, but it floated out of her like sparks from a fire, rising up from her mom to float away.

Her mom was sick. She could feel the sickness in Alice like a black writhing mass. The doctors had so many words for what was wrong with her: so many words, so many explanations, reasons, and no solutions.

Teri knew. She could taste her mom and knew her time was done, that her power had run its course.

Standing in a room in the same hospital that Teri had been years before back from the dead, she watched her mother's energy disperse into the world around, becoming a part of all things once again.

She turned from the husk that had been her mother and walked out of the hospital and walked among trees, feeling her mother in every leaf and branch of every tree. She walked with her mother until she'd become a part of the world.

Later, after the funeral, Teri met her aunt. She had heard about her strange aunt that lived in Accord in the little house right on the edge of the village, but she had never met her. Something had happened between her mother and aunt a long time ago, and they never spoke.

Teri was standing alone dressed in black when the aunt walked up to her and said, "Hi Teri. I'm sorry for your loss. I'm your aunt Sharon.

Teri looked up at the tall slim woman with very long grey

hair loose to her waist. Teri turned and smiled, "It's nice to meet you," she extended her hand, "I'm Teri."

Sharon looked at the extended hand, smiled, looked up at Teri, "I knows you is, little one."

She looked at Teri for a long minute. "Looks like I should have come to see you sooner." She paused and looked down. "Guess I know when it happened. I read you died, then you were alive again. A lot of confusion around you. You seem to have found your way, though, but I could have probably helped some."

Sharon reached out and took Teri's hand. Her hand was warm and dry, a bit dry but no power. Just a hand, nothing more.

Sharon smiled, 'were you expecting sumthin more?" She winked.

Teri looked at Sharon.

"Why don't you stop by for tea next week?" Sharon asked.

"Sure. That would be perfect." Teri said.

The next week Teri drove into Accord and looked for Sharon's little house. She knew more or less where it was. With only 19 streets in the village, it wasn't difficult to find. It was in the north of the village, and backed on to a large, protected forest.

It was a pretty house, painted a light blue and white.

Teri parked in front and walked to the front door. As she approached the front door, she heard Sharon's voice from around the back of the house, "Out here. Come around the right side through the gate."

Teri walked around the house through the gate and walked into a paradise. It was a garden like she had never seen.

At once wild and untamed, but that was a carefully planned look. It had been meticulously considered and laid out.

Teri marvelled at the diversity of plant life growing in profusion everywhere. She soon realized this was not an ornamental garden. It was very pretty, but this was a garden with a purpose.

Each plant and flower had its very specific use, and each had been chosen with careful intent. Some plants she knew, many she did not. She knew willow bark, garlic, self-heal, feverfew, willow and lavender. She knew how to use sage, peppermint, goosegrass boneset and dandelion. These were common enough. Some even her mom had known, but there were plants in this garden she had never seen before.

"Welcome," Sharon said as she stood up from gathering plants in a plastic bin on the ground beside her. Once again, Teri admired the grace with which Sharon moved. She moved like a much younger woman. She had been Teri's mom's older sister, which put her in her early 70's.

"What are you smiling about, little one?" Sharon said.

Teri didn't reply. She closed her eyes and opened herself to the garden and to Sharon. Immediately she was flooded with stories, volumes of emotions. She allowed herself to fill with the power that surrounded her. The garden was a maze of power, an intricate design even more carefully planned than Teri had first thought. Feeling it revealed that it had been designed with power in mind, for the collection and storage of energy of every conceivable type. When Teri turned her attention to Sharon, she found a hole, a blank space that she could not feel.

Teri knew Sharon was right there in front of her. When she felt for her with the power, she was a blank spot in the world, a Sharon-shaped blank spot.

"My, my. You are very powerful, indeed. Come, let's go

in for a spell and have tea. I've been in the sun all morn and need a sit-down." Sharon said.

They walked around to the back door of the little house.

The door was open with no screen door. They walked through, Sharon pausing to slip off her boots.

They were standing in a walled porch with a large many-panelled window along one side. Under the window was a table that ran the length of the porch. The table was covered in potted plants of every description. Teri recognized none of them.

Teri followed Sharon, who padded barefoot, into a large room that was the house's main room. It had a wood-burning stove almost in the middle of the room. It was sparsely decorated with two broken-down, comfortable-looking armchairs draped in blankets, a harvest table with a couple of wooden chairs covered in books and papers, and a heavily weighed- down bookcase in the corner.

Teri breathed in when she felt the raw, bright power that pulsed from the books and papers. Some books vibrated where they sat, excited to reveal their secrets. Some amber and gold, others more jewel-toned, they glowed with energy and welcome.

Sharon watched Teri closely, appraising, measuring, observing.

"Sit," Sharon said as she went into the small kitchen and busied herself getting a heavy black pot on the stove.

Teri sat in one of the chairs. It curled around her protectively. She felt safe and warm.

After a second, Sharon returned and sat opposite Teri. "So, Teri. I see you have a bit of understanding of the power within you." Sharon said, her glance indicating the bookshelf.

"I... yes, I guess I do. I mean, I do," Teri said.

Sharon looked at her, studied her. "You saw your mom's death.

Oh, wait." Sharon said, rising to take the whistling pot off the stove. She returned with a teapot and two mugs swinging at her side.

"Yes," Teri said.

Sharon sat and smiled at Teri. "I saw it as well. I saw you too. I felt your birth. I saw the moment the power touched you. I saw you accept it. I felt the wind shift and the earth quiver." Sharon poured tea into each of the mugs and offered one to Teri.

Teri took the mug and looked at Sharon, waiting for her to continue.

Sharon sat and sipped her tea, looking at Teri. Teri looked at her mug, then took a sip. It was very good tea. Teri could recognize some of the ingredients. Chamomile, lavender, lemon balm, passionflower, holy basil and turmeric were easy, but there was something else.

"Hops, licorice, and St. John's wort," Sharon said as if answering a question Teri hadn't asked.

Teri nodded, letting the tea do its work. She relaxed as the warmth of the tea filled her. She looked at the tea then opened herself to it. The tea was full of power. It swelled inside her, swirling with colour.

Sharon smiled at Teri's obvious pleasure at the tea.

"So beautiful," Teri said, watching the colours spin in and out of her mug.

After a minute, she asked, "Why are you hiding from me?"

"Hiding?" Sharon asked over her mug. They sat quietly for a time. Teri watched Sharon with the power.

"Ok, yes, I'm masking myself from you. I didn't expect you to be as strong as you are." Sharon leaned back in her chair and looked into her mug, "I was a little older than you when I received the power. Something had happened," she paused, "I went to the crossroads and sold my soul to have the power to take vengeance. The Judge gave me something I never expected. I'm embarrassed now to say I did not take to the power, like you. I did some horrible things before I found balance."

Teri watched with the power as slowly Sharon revealed herself.

"I was so angry. I hurt people, some very badly. I hurt your mother. Not with the power but with words. She never really forgave me, and I don't blame her. Now it's no longer important." Sharon looked down.

Teri could see Sharon now. She glowed brighter than anyone Teri had ever looked at. Sharon's power was massive. It eclipsed anything Teri had thought possible, but there was a dark spot right at the center of Sharon's being. A large dark hole as if a fire had burned out the middle of her, leaving a blackened carved out area that seemed to radiate dark, cold and complete.

Teri pulled back from it with a gasp.

"Yes, that is my shame. Part of it is something I created, and some of it grew from where the power came from. I had only one task to complete for the Judge, but that was enough for me. What he asked of me did not seem too bad on the surface, but now, in hindsight, I realize how terrible it was."

Teri watched Sharon's power waver. It was then Teri saw what Sharon had been hiding.

She was dying. Teri watched Sharon. The energy in her pulsed, never changing, but her body was worn thin, like skin drawn too tightly across bones. She would be dead soon, very soon.

"Ah, you see." Sharon said, "Yes, my time is near. I have

known for some time, but now there is so little time to give you all I need to give you."

Sharon rose, "Come, I have something for you."
She crossed the room to the bookcase and pulled down a large handmade book with a thin wood cover and heavy pages. This book glowed with rainbows of power.

"This will give you much of what you need to take care of the garden and this house. I am leaving this all to you. It is my seat of power, and it will become yours. You will need it if what I see in your future is true."

"My future?" Teri asked.

Sharon smiled, "Yes, with enough focus, some futures can be glimpsed. It is not very accurate, but the touch can be helpful. Here." She handed the book to Teri, who took it carefully in both hands.

She held it for a moment, then looked at Sharon, then opened herself to the book and pulled the words into herself.
Now it was Sharon's turn to gasp, "I had a glimpse of that possibility, but I never thought it would be that powerful."
Teri looked up. Her eyes shone with the new knowledge that poured into her.

"Maybe this won't be as difficult as I feared," Sharon said and smiled, impressed.

Sharon gestured to her books and papers. Teri stepped forward, eager to draw in the knowledge, eager for the warmth to flood her. She extended her hands, touching the books and paper lightly.

The amount of power stored here arched her back, bending her spine till her head was thrown back, and she gasped at the sheer volume of power.

After a time, her head came forward. White sparks danced around her fingers, around her eyelashes. She was floating inches off the floor. Teri turned to Sharon and smiled. She glowed brightly, and Sharon, mouth open, stared at Teri.

From then on, Teri visited every day. They worked in the garden, talked about the magics, and drank tea. Teri found she liked Sharon for the most part, but there was a side that Sharon kept secret, locked away. A place Sharon would never reveal nor talk about. Teri knew it was there. Saw its shadow in Sharon. It had something to do with the Judge, but that is as far as she knew.

A few weeks later, Sharon died. She, like her sister, died as she had lived. The only difference was that where Teri's mom had been gentle, Sharon was not.

They were sitting in the garden, talking quietly when the day came.

"Teri. Have a life. Get married, have kids, get a dog. I don't know. Just have a life. Whatever a 'life' means to you. Don't let the power take that away from you. I let it rule me. It's no good." Sharon said.

When the time came Sharon smiled. Teri opened herself to the power. She watched as Sharon separated from her power. Her power flashed bright white and spread out. She exploded. The shock wave rocketed outward, then crashed back, and Sharon was gone.

The man that came to visit stepped into the garden radiating with darkness. It was late on a fine spring afternoon. She was sitting in Sharon's garden. Even after all these years, she still looked around at the garden and saw Sharon's hand. The garden told her he was coming.

He walked around the house through the gate, dressed

in a fine dark suit and smiling. The garden flinched as he slowly walked along the path toward Teri.

She hadn't seen him since the night he gifted her the power, but his presence was everywhere she went. His poison had spread through the area in an expanding black cloud. With her sight, she could see 'the marked' as they went about their day. She could see the ash on their forehead, a burnt spot where their soul once could look out at the world, now blinded and destined to belong to the Judge.

The Judge smiled his perfectly polished smile.

"Teri, my girl. How have you been?"

Teri sat very still, watching him walk through the garden, a small creature in the presence of a predator.

"I was right. You have become very powerful." He looked at her, "Yes, very powerful."

He looked around the garden, "I can feel her here still, in places. I saw when she released the power. She had been such a good servant." He surveyed the garden and house, "It was nice. She left this for you."

Teri sat very still. She could feel his power. It was vastly deeper than her own, a well of darkness the depth of which she could never have fathomed. She probed, looking for something. With herself open, she pushed at the edges of him, looking for a weak spot. She found none.

"You don't have to do that. We are not enemies. How could we be? You are of me. The power that flows through you is of me, from me. I gave it to you. I am your creator. There is no need to fight me. Besides, I only have one small request of you, this day. A tiny thing."

Calmly, Teri continued looking in the shadows of this creature. "I am not of you," she said. There was something, something he was hiding. She could see that. Things were not as she had first thought. He had a secret. Something that shone like silver, silver coins, maybe. It was fuzzy.

The Judge sensed her probe. He closed himself.

"Teri. Teri. Why do you insist on pushing back?" The Judge stepped forward, smiling, "What do you possibly think is going to happen? Sharon was one of the most powerful servants I have ever known. You are not Sharon. She did as she was asked. Yes, she had her moments, but in the end, she did as she was bidden, even if she hated herself for it."

Teri started pulling in power. She was grateful she was barefooted. Her toes dug into the grass. She would have to pull in as much as fast as she could before he saw. She gathered around herself. Making a wall around herself to draw on when it was time.

"Yer gran used to say, 'if yer dog bites you, there was a lead pill for that'. I don't want to have to put you down."

She shoved herself upright to a standing position and completely opened her being. She reached down into the earth, not to the earth itself. That she could not do but to the thousands of tiny creatures below her. She pulled, hearing, regretting their sacrifice. She pulled like she had never done before.

She ignored the rising blackness in front of her and reached out to the garden. She stretched herself out and pulled all the stored power there, years of power stored by her and by Sharon before her. It rushed into her, filling her.

She wasn't sure she could contain the power she gathered, but she knew it was just for a heartbeat.

As powerful as she was, the black mass in front of her dwarfed her tiny light.

When the dark touched the edges of her, she flinched. It burned not of heat, but of cold. A cold so deep and vast it seemed it would erase everything.

As fast as she could with every ounce of strength she had built up over the years since she lay on that cold pavement, she pulled in power. She reached further out, touching on the house. Reaching into the house to the books and papers there, pulling from them the stored power that still hid within those pages.

Further still, she reached across the street and pulled power from the neighbour's dog, from a mouse that ran along the side of the garage, from a passing hawk, making it falter in the air before it flew on.

With all the gathered power, she pushed back and knew instantly it would not be enough, not nearly enough.

The darkness that bore down on her was as vast as the depth of an ocean, deep and black. Its resources were unlimited. This creature had the power of Hell behind it. How could she possibly prevail against such an ancient power?

She pushed harder, unleashing everything, and felt herself fail. She began to shrink under the black. She thought of Sharon and how she, too, failed. She thought of her mother and how she never touched the power she could have had. She felt her mother then, just a small warm nugget inside her. She saw her mother's first smile at her when she was just born. It was slightly blurred, viewed with brand new eyes, but the pure, honest joy shone from them. The warmth in her grew. She felt the hug of her mother in the kitchen for no reason other than to share love, and she felt the darkness pause.

She saw Sharon, who had bequeathed everything she had, even her power. She remembered Sharon's last words to her.

"Get a life."

Teri had smiled, knowing that that wasn't in the cards for her. Knowing she would live alone in the house Sharon had built, waiting for this day, the day The Judge came to take from her. And now that it had come, she felt for the dream that Sharon had given her.

Yes, her life would be filled with love and acceptance, just not in the way Sharon had seen. Teri stopped pushing and opened herself. She opened to the power below. She opened herself to the earth. She touched what terrified her. The power that rested below her, so massive it overwhelmed everything. A planet-sized power that she feared just because of its sheer immensity, but when she accepted the power, sure that it would be her end, she found she was wrong. It did not simply wash over her. It did not erase her. It embraced her. The gentle power slipped warmth around her. She felt the warmth, felt the acceptance and love fill her.

She knew nothing could touch her. She was safe.

The blackness flinched and pulled back. The dark surged forward, slamming into her with no effect. Teri stood in the middle of a great swirling black void, untouched, wrapped in a power greater than the dark.
Suddenly the dark receded and vanished.

When Teri's feet touched the grass, it crackled dryly. She opened her eyes. The Judge was gone, not defeated but refused for now.

Teri looked around at the garden. Her spring garden, with all its fresh bright green, was now brown as winter. She had taken almost its all. She walked carefully among the brown dry plants, feeling their fragile burnt stalks and leaves. She cried for what she had done.

The power of the garden was gone. Burnt up in the second of pushing, it would take years to regrow it, and some things would never return. They were of Sharon, and Teri had no knowledge of them.

She slipped to her knees and touched the brown grass. Tentatively she reached out, opening herself. It was difficult. Before, she could open herself like opening her hand, now she struggled to find the mechanism. She managed to open herself in a small way. She could feel the power. It was distant and faint, but it was there. She searched around herself. In the ground, she could feel the small creatures trying to recover from the onslaught she had inflicted upon them. She was grateful only a few had died.

After a few moments, she rose and went in. She put on the kettle and looked at her books and papers, now blank and void of any power. These she had drained completely. She felt sadness at the loss. There would be no return for these. The magic was no longer in the books and no longer in her.

Some of the magic was still in her, buried deep. She could feel it even if she could not access it. That, too, would take time.

The kettle boiled. She poured herself a tea and sat in one of the comfy chairs.

The tea was also weakened, but it was warm and still had a small amount of the power she needed. She sipped and smiled at her future, now really hers, at least for a while.

# CHAPTER 6

## THE TOUCH

Adam was obsessed with green and growing things. He would lay on the lawn, his face deep into the grass. He could hear the grass grow, hear the tiny clicks and soft scraping sounds. Slowly, the world revealed itself to him. He watched as small creatures, some with surprisingly bright colours, came out of hiding. There were creatures with shells of vibrant red and yellow, yet invisible to everyone–even to him until he stopped to see.

In his mind's eye, he would walk through this world, climbing over stalks of grass wider than he was, ducking under fall's dead grass and confronting creatures so large that he was just a tiny bug in front of them. He would imagine riding a tiny red ant like a man riding a horse, a horse that could climb vertical stalks of grass. Hours passed, lost in the miniature world he found.

Years later, Adam worked as the produce manager at Safeway. It was a job he loved. In high school he had worked as a bag boy, and after he graduated he went full time. It was only a few years and he was made produce manager. He loved being around fresh vegetables. He loved their colours, their crispness. He loved the Life.

When the store was empty, he would walk around his department and smell, just smell. Sometimes he would press his face into the lettuce or cabbage to immerse himself in the Life. The scent brought him back to a time when he was quite young - a time of getting lost.

Adam's life was just about perfect. He had a job he truly loved. He was around green things all day long. The only thing he could wish for was a spot to grow things himself, maybe a deck with some planters or perhaps a garden. He couldn't afford a house, not in the city, certainly not on his salary, but maybe a condo with a deck or a rooftop patio.

He contacted a realtor to discuss buying a more suitable condo. He'd sell his and move up. But the realtor frowned as he walked through Adam's small condo. Then he turned and smiled broadly. Of course, he could help him sell his current condo and find another, but he would have to be realistic. His condo was in an older building in an area that hadn't gentrified as fast as others, so what he wanted would be more money.

With a polished smile that dazzled Adam, the realtor explained to him what he actually wanted. In Adam's mind, the vision blossomed like the garden he would surely have. The realtor would run some numbers, do some searches and get back to him. They shook hands, Adam feeling happier than he had for years.

A couple of days later, Adam got a call from his realtor that popped his bubble. He was very sorry, but his situation had changed, and he had decided to leave the real estate business. However, if Adam was still interested, he could recommend a realtor who would help him.

The realtor said, "His name is Ol' Tom, and he is the very best in the city. He is in extremely high demand, but he also is a close personal friend that had made all my dreams come true and would take you on as a favour to me."

Adam had seen the signs around town with Ol' Tom's name, but he couldn't remember what he looked like. After a pause, he said, "Absolutely, I'm very interested! That would be great."

"There's one small thing because of how busy he is. He can only meet you at midnight tomorrow evening. I know it's late, but it's his only opening for several weeks."

"Will he have any time for me if he's that busy?"

Adam was starting to feel unsure about the whole affair.

"Oh, yes. He has a multitude of assistants. You will get service like I could never have given you. Believe me. He is connected like no one you will ever meet. He is very special. You won't regret it."

"OK, well, alright," Adam smiled, "Ya sure... Sure, I can meet him. Here at the condo?"

"No, meet him at Preston Avenue and College Drive." Adam chuckled, "Isn't that a busy corner to be meeting at?"

"Not at midnight." After a pause, the ex-realtor said, "It's not far from your place."

"No, not bad. OK, I'll be there." Adam hung up the phone.

He was standing in his kitchen and he couldn't remember what he had been doing before the phone call. He stood for minutes, long minutes. He looked around the kitchen. He looked at the stove. Was I cooking? Was it supper time? He looked at the clock on the stove. 6:66? It couldn't be. There was no time displayed, just a number. He stared at the clock. No, it was 6:36. He chuckled at himself. Why was he feeling so weird? So off? He felt like he was waking from a long deep sleep, foggy and a head packed with cotton balls. He stared at the clock. 6:37. Yes, supper. That's what I need. He just needed to eat something. That's what he'd been doing. He looked around the kitchen. He couldn't see any sign he had started prepping for any food.

He stood for a few more long moments, then decided he wasn't hungry, walked into the living room and sat. To his left, he looked out the window that overlooked the city. The window faced east. He saw some amazing sunrises, or rather he had when he'd first bought the condo. Back then, he could see straight across the city all the way to downtown. Now the city had sprouted numerous new condo buildings. Every other day, it seemed, another building sprung from a hole in the ground like a glass and steel weed blocking the sky and his sunrises.

He stood in the center of his front room, rooted to the spot, and looked unseeing through the window, thinking about sunrises and bugs. With a jerk, he realized he was staring at a dark nighttime sky. It had been early evening, just a second ago, hadn't it? He was confused. There was a distance in his mind. Again he felt like he had just woken from sleep. Or maybe he was still asleep and dreaming. Dreaming of being awake.

He looked at the lit windows of the condos across from him. He could see people moving about above and below each other, unaware of how close they were. He watched a heavy naked man smoke by an open window, scratching himself. Right above him, a woman in a robe ironed a blouse. Below him, a man played video games. He watched them for a while, lost in their small bubbles they knew as their lives. Just another Wednesday night, like a hundred others.

"I guess I should get going," he said to the empty apartment. He felt it was time. He turned and left his bubble.

The apartment was dark. He didn't close the door. Just stepped out into the hallway, down the stairs and out into the street.

The coolness of the evening surprised him. He walked without thinking, calm, relaxed, not a worry in his mind. He strolled, knowing he would be on time. He watched people in their bubbles, doing whatever it was they were doing, going where they were going, unaware of him, unaware of anything outside of their bubbles.

Absently he noticed that there were not that many people out, fewer than he would have expected. When he realized that, he stopped and looked around. As he neared the crossroads he was heading for, there were fewer and fewer people. It was surreal, like a 60's sci-fi movie. The streetlights lit the empty streets.

When he arrived, he walked to the middle of the crossroads and stood still. He turned on the spot. There wasn't a person to be seen, no lights of cars. It was eerie. The strangeness rattled him, and he lost some of the fog that had wrapped around his head right after the phone call about this meeting.

He remembered hearing on the radio a couple of months back that this intersection was the deadliest crossroads in the city, in the country.

Far off, he could hear the city hum. The life of the city continued, but here there was nothing. He was startled by the sound of tires right behind him. He spun and saw a long black car pull up close. He stared.

The door opened, and a tall, thin man stepped out onto the pavement. He was dressed in a fine black suit. He gave off an air of pristine calmness, a relaxed confidence that he wore with utter assurance. He smiled at Adam. It was a perfect smile. It was polished chrome, fixed and focused, glinting with predatory intensity. Adam shrank back.

The man stepped forward, hand extended. "Mr. Gardner, How very nice to meet you."

Adam paused, unsure. Then he shook the proffered hand.

"Ol' Tom?" Adam felt silly calling this man Ol' Tom. He was not an "Ol' Tom", he was a shark, not a friendly, back-home kinda guy.

"Yes," he said. His smile widened as if he knew the name didn't match the face, and continued, "Excellent. And why do you wish to move, if I may ask?"

"I'm tired of the city. I want a larger place I…"

"Yes… yes, but what is it you truly want?" Ol' Tom interrupted. "What do you want in your heart? What is it deep down that you want?"

He looked at Adam. His eyes bore into him. They grew, expanded, becoming universes of black. Adam stared into them. He got lost. The fog that had blanketed his brain earlier in the day now thickened and tightened. He felt himself fall. Or nearly fall, like the moment of falling asleep. A sudden jerk that usually wakes. It didn't wake him. The gravity of those eyes pulled him into them.

His heart opened, and he said, "I want to grow life." And then they were standing on the pavement in the city at the crossroads of Preston and College, two men talking. The tall man in the black suit smiled, and it was almost a friendly smile that nearly reached his eyes.

"Life? Well, Adam. That's a biggie," he rubbed his chin.

"You know, I don't think I've had this request before." He laughed. "I do believe I can give you that."

For a second Adam looked at him, a vagueness in his eyes, he shook his head and the fog that had clamped down on him lifted. He looked around, at the street, the city lights, and at Ol' Tom.

"Ah. I'm sorry, what were we talking about?"

"Oh, we were just discussing your housing needs. I think I can help you."

"Yes. That's great," Adam smiled, still somewhat confused.

Ol' Tom turned, paused and said like an afterthought, "Adam, would you mind signing this representation agreement? Totally standard."

"Well, of course," Adam said smiling, and signed the paper.

The walk home seemed much longer. Adam felt elated, as though something momentous had just happened. He walked with a lightness in his step, looking around the city, watching the people in their bubbles walking to destinations unknown to him. He felt right, as if the world agreed with him for the first time in his life.

He would move to a new home where he could watch life, life he brought into the world. He could watch it flourish and dazzle him as he had when he was young and the small world opened to him in the grass.

A week went by, and Adam's excitement grew. He started looking at gardening magazines, videos, and seeking out websites with horticultural advice. While Adam was obsessed with plants and the growing things, he had never actually planted anything, had never had a houseplant. In some ways, he felt that to have a house plant was like putting a plant in prison. Was it right to keep the plant locked away from the air and light that was its natural environment? He didn't look down on people, at least not too much, for having house plants. It just wasn't what he wanted to do. It just wasn't right.

He hadn't heard from Ol' Tom for almost a week, then in the late afternoon he heard a knock on the door. Standing there in the hallway was an incredibly tall man in a dark suit and a large-brimmed hat. He had a smile like Ol' Tom's, huge and broad except where Ol' Tom's was so white it dazzled, this smile was a sickly grey. For an uncomfortable moment, Adam was sure he saw a flickering movement beneath the surface of the teeth, like a larva under a thin translucent shell. Adam shivered and looked away. When he looked back, the teeth were white and the smile even broader.

"I am Mr. September."

"Mr. September. That's an unusual name," Adam said unthinkingly. He immediately regretted saying it.

The man, Mr. September, smiled and said, "Yes. I am here in Ol' Tom's stead." His left hand came up, holding a black leather book. After a quick glance, he looked back to Adam.

"He has found you a new home."

Adam stared at him, not understanding, "I'm sorry. What did you say?"

"He has found you a new home," Mr. September said as though it was the most beautiful thing.

"I…" he paused. "He found me a home?"

"Yes, a NEW home." He smiled, "Ol' Tom said to tell you this is the perfect home for you."

"I haven't looked at anything yet. Isn't that the way it works? I go and look at places till I find one I like, then I put in an offer."

The man in the hat seemed puzzled.

Adam noticed he could not see the man's eyes. He looked at the dark under the brim, trying to see them. He shivered, a dread he could not put his finger on, touched his spine. Mr. September's smile faltered slightly, as if he was aware of Adam's discomfort, then it came back brighter than ever.

"Yes, that is the normal way. However, Ol' Tom purchased

118

the new property knowing you would love it. Would you like to see it?"

"Hum? Yes, I guess."

"That's just the bee's knees," the man in the hat said. It sounded like something he had heard and was trying out.

"What?"

The smile diminished slightly, "That's great," he said without enthusiasm.

Adam looked at Mr. September, feeling like he was in a dream where things looked right, but they were not. Everything about this man was off.

"Umm. Where is this new place?" Adam said.

The man's smile grew impossibly large. He seemed relieved to be on solid ground again. "It is at 792 Cartwright Street. It's in the Willows."

Adam thought it sounded weird, as though the address was supposed to be a source of pride.

"Here are the keys."

Adam took the keys and looked at them. House keys. Just house keys with a small cardboard tag tied with a string. It read 792 Cartwright St in a barely readable scrawl.

"OK. Am I going to meet Ol' Tom there or what?"

After a pause, the man said, "No," his smile frozen on his face. They stood still staring at each other for a long minute. Adam wasn't sure what to do. He decided the conversation was over. He said "OK," and closed the door. Adam stood for a moment listening, then opened the door. The man was gone. Adam stepped out a bit and looked down the hallway. The man was nowhere to be seen. He turned and looked at the window. Flies buzzed about, banging against the glass. The casement and the floor beneath the window were covered in dead black flies.

He stepped further into the hallway, looking at the hundreds of black flies strewn across the windowsill and carpet. They were all dead and dying. He couldn't remember ever seeing such a sight. It mesmerized him as it repulsed him. It was the same feeling he had with plants. From decay came life. He kneeled and peered down at the black mass. Some flies were still moving, their legs twitching, an occasional flutter of their plastic-looking wings.

He leaned closer, his face inches from the heaps. The smell wasn't unpleasant. In fact, there was the same smell of earth and life he was always searching for. He closed his eyes and breathed deep. The scent filled him. He stood and swayed.

When he opened his eyes, he was no longer standing in the hallway outside of his apartment door. Before him, in the dark, the black sand stretched out as far as he could see. It seemed to shimmer in the light that came from the stars, ...stars?

He looked up at the near-black sky. It was strewn with white stars that didn't feel like stars. They were too consistent, too bright, and there were far too many of them. They filled the sky from horizon to horizon and ended at what looked like a far-off range of mountains that really could only be seen by the absence of those same stars.

He realized he was cold. He wrapped his arms around himself and looked around. He was standing not far from a river. It was black and flowed slowly. Shivering, he turned and walked towards it.

On a whim, he turned and looked back at his tracks. The smooth black sand was unmarked. He took a step backward and watched as the sand erased the impressions his feet had left.

He turned back to the river and stopped on the bank,

looking across the smooth water. It reflected the stars, stretching and pulling them in its currents and eddies.

He looked up and down the river. There was nothing to be seen. He turned right and started to walk.

He could not have said how long he walked. The cold was deep inside him now. He had stopped shivering, but he knew he was cold. He looked back the way he had come. There was no trace he had ever walked there.

He looked up at the stars. Their light was icy, a white that made him feel the cold. He clenched his teeth to stop them from chattering. His jaw muscles hurt from the effort.

He continued to walk, head down. As he walked, he tried to remember the dates of things. He counted his steps and when he lost count, he would restart. He stumbled and realized he had no idea how far he had come. He was convinced he had been asleep as he walked.

He shook his head and continued on, with no idea where he was or where he was going, but he felt he had to continue. He didn't know how long he walked till he stumbled again. This time he fell forward, his arm splashing in the river's edge.
He pulled back violently. It felt like the water had tugged at him. He looked at his arm. It wasn't wet. Where his arm had touched the water, there was a small eddy. He was sure it was his imagination or just that he was so tired, but it looked for a second like the water bulged. He felt menace and moved back. The eddy disappeared.

He stood looking at the river, holding his arm. To his right, still some distance away, there was something. A shape that broke the constant landscape. He walked toward it. It did not disappear as he feared it might. Instead, it grew with each step. He moved quicker.

He squinted, working to make it out. It was a structure,

but what kind he wasn't sure. It looked like a fence or maybe a low building with lots of windows.

He slowed when he realized he was looking at a huge pier that jutted out over the river. It amazed him how long it took to reach it. It was much larger than he had first thought. Without something to measure it against, it looked large, but he never would have guessed just how massive it was.

The road that led away from the pier was hard-packed black sand. He noticed along both sides were dark shapes half-buried in the sand. He examined the nearest shape. He was only a couple of paces from it when he knew what he was looking at. It was a suitcase, half-open, its contents scattered, beside it was another, this one closed and partially buried. He looked around. There was stuff everywhere. Beside the suitcases, there was clothing of all kinds, packages, boxes, laptops, even toys and phones, hundreds of shiny small rectangles scattered about, along the side of the road.

He walked several paces, just looking at the sheer volume of detritus, when a whitish object caught his eyes. He stared, not wanting to get any closer, knowing instinctively what he was looking at but denying it nonetheless. In spite of himself, he moved a step closer and knew he was looking at the small skull of a child partially wrapped in a blanket. Reluctantly he lifted his head and looked down the roadside. The white shapes seemed to pop out at him.

He decided that he was dreaming. He hadn't thought about the weirdness and horror of all this. He had just accepted it. It was a dream, and with that clear in his head, it was OK. He would just see what would happen next. Eventually he'd wake, and this would be over. With dream logic, he turned and walked back and out on the pier.

He noticed the sound as he stepped from sand to pier.

His foot made a hollow thump. He realized how quiet it had been. There was no sound. No wind, no animals, not even sounds from the river. Just the sounds he brought with him. His breathing, the rustle of his clothes, even his heart beating. Now foot-falls on the pier.

He walked softly trying to be quiet as if he was in a grand old library or in a church at a funeral.

The pier was made of massive timbers, black and hard with age. They were worn. Each plank was cupped by thousands of feet that had walked on them.

He looked back down the road with the strewn suitcases and abandoned stuff. Thousands of feet that dropped their belongings... he stopped himself. He didn't want to think about that.

Turning back, he walked further along the pier. It was wide, easily as wide as a street. On each side was a railing made of large wooden beams. He angled himself as he walked and came up to the nearest railing. The wood was old and black here as well, but it was not worn. No hands had touched it. No one had stood and looked out at the dark landscape. Leaning forward he looked at the slowly moving water. He was surprised at how far down it was. A grid work of massive black timbers supported the pier. Where they touched the water, it seemed to pull back from the wood and created tiny eddies that spiralled slowly away.

He straightened and continued down the pier. At the end, the railing stopped at the left-hand side while the right continued, then turned and closed off the end. Here, large mooring anchors were bolted to the wood. Something large docked here. He looked up and down the river, then across to the other side. For the first time, he could make out the other side. There was another large pier across and upriver from where he stood.

He noticed movement and realized there was a man standing on the pier looking back at him. This was the first person he had seen since entering this dream. Adam waved, moving his arms in big swinging movements. He was sure the man saw him, but he made no response and just stood looking. He stopped waving. The man on the other pier turned and walked away. Adam cursed quietly.

Adam watched the reflection of the stars twist in the river's current. He looked down into the black water and saw his face reflected there. For a dizzying second he felt as if he fell then he was standing looking at his face in a mirror. It was dark. He was in the bathroom in his condo with the lights off.

He pulled back and looked around. It must have been a dream. He was sleepwalking. He had never walked in his sleep before. He flipped the light on and couldn't understand what he saw in the mirror. He had the beginnings of a beard, at least a couple days' growth. He rubbed his face and left the bathroom. He found his phone, but it was dead. He flipped the tv on and went to the weather channel. It was 6 days since the afternoon the strange man in the black suit had shown up with the "keys to his new home."

He sat on the couch and looked at the TV. He felt tired. How could I be tired? Didn't I just wake up? He let his head tip back and fell instantly asleep.

He woke with sunlight pouring in the window. His neck hurt. He had slept without moving and without dreaming. He had slept for hours, but he still felt tired. He felt fuzzy, like his head was wrapped in a fog that he couldn't shake.

He picked up his phone. He was glad he had plugged it in before he fell asleep. He turned it on. There were 28 missed calls, all of them from work. Of course, he had missed a lot of work with no explanation.

Shit. It was 9:40. He should have already been at work for a couple of hours. He dialled the office number. Jerry, the manager, answered on the second ring.

"Yes?"

"Hey, Jer," Adam couldn't keep the apology out of his voice.

"Adam! How are you feeling? Christ, I was worried!"

"I… why… what do you mean?"

"Well, fuck Adam. You disappear for days. No reason. No call. I was going to call the cops. Then you called."

"I called?"

"Ya, if you can call that a call. It was truly bizarre. You must have been running a fever. All you said was I can't make it. I just can't make it. It was weird. And the connection was screwed up. All crackly, and your voice was like it was a thousand miles away."

Adam frowned, trying to figure what had happened. Did I call when I was sleeping?

"Adam?" Jerry's voice sounded worried. "Are you still sick?"

"I'm better, but still not a 100%."

"You don't sound good. Take the time you need." Jerry had already moved on and wasn't listening.

"Thanks, Jer. I'll call."

He hung up. He thought about Jerry, overweight and always drinking coke. He was more than ten years younger but looked ten years older than Adam.

Adam walked to the washroom. Well, I used to look younger than Jerry. His skin was ashy. There were dark circles under his eyes. He licked his dry and cracked lips. He stripped off his clothes and showered. After he had dried, he walked to the bedroom and pulled on jeans and a T-shirt.

In the living room, he looked around. His clothes were in a pile in the doorway to the bathroom. He should pick them up, he thought, then he pulled on his Converse and left.

In half an hour, he was driving along Cartwright looking for 792. There were some fine houses. He was sure he couldn't afford a house here, no matter how good Ol' Tom was.

When he found the address, it was carved into a rock; he turned into the curving lane. He definitely couldn't afford this. He drove up the lane, past the stone, past a stand of trees, and there was one of the most beautiful houses he had ever seen.

It was a modern bungalow, a cubist sculpture of cement, iron and glass. He stopped in front and pulled out the key Mr. September had given him and looked at the tag, "792 Cartwright". There must be another Cartwright. He looked at the tag again and got out of the car. He walked to the door and, half expecting it not to fit, slid the key in. It turned easily. He frowned and pushed the door open.

Inside, it was even more beautiful than outside. The glass, cement and dark wood continued. He stood on a dark red Persian carpet. The ceiling in the foyer was high. To his right was a spare living room with leather couches. To his left was a dining table of glass and chrome. Beyond that was a large kitchen full of chrome and black marble. He couldn't believe how gorgeous this house was.

No one lived here. There was nothing to suggest that anyone had. In the kitchen, he looked out at the backyard. The yard was equally beautiful, perfectly manicured, but what caught his eyes and held them was the massive glass greenhouse that stretched from the kitchen to the end of the property.

He could smell the earth and the green growing things,

and his heart rejoiced. His pace quickened. He burst into the great greenhouse. It had large flat planting beds running the entire length of the house. They were filled with rich black soil, and in the ground were small green leaves standing proud and full of life. He looked at the life that was here. This is where he wanted to be. This is where he belonged. He still had trouble believing Ol' Tom could find such a place that was in his price range, but here he was and he wasn't leaving.

Slowly he walked along the beds, looking at his charges on both sides of him. He was almost halfway down when a loud crack to his right made him turn. A black shape had slammed into an upper glass panel, cracking it. At first, he didn't know what it was, but as it slid and fell to the ground, he saw that it was a dead crow. He walked closer and stared at it through the glass. He looked up at the cracked pane.

"Good morning, Adam." The voice came from his left. He spun. A man stood deep in the greenhouse. He was a tall, slim black man dressed all in black, a clean suit over a turtleneck sweater with his hair stacked and flat-topped. He smiled. He had a forked goatee and perfect teeth.

"I thought I would visit your home, since you visited mine."

"I'm sorry, who are you?" Adam stood still as the man started to walk toward him, his hands outstretched, brushing the tops of the small delicate leaves. They withered and browned as he touched them.

"Stop that!" Adam didn't know how he was killing his plants, but they were his responsibility, "Stop that." Adam took a step forward.

The man stopped and brought his hands together in front of himself. "Yes, I suppose that would upset you. It's my nature. I am a collector, you see."

127

"A collector? Who are you, and what are you doing in my home?"

"Your home? Really? Well, this is a truly fine home." He looked at the greenhouse and smiled. "Yes, a fine home."

"Look, mister. Who are you?"

"You may call me Mr. White." He smiled.

"Mr. White...? What kind of name is that? That sounds like a fake name." Adam was nervous and wasn't sure why, making him angry, and his words came out sharply. This was an intruder in his home. 'In his home?' He had been here less than an hour, and he was calling it 'his home.'

"Hmmm? It may be to your ears. Really, it's not terribly important what you call me. It is important that you realize who I am."

"I don't care who you are. You are trespassing, and I want you gone." Adam stood as tall as he could, puffing his chest up. Even still, he was nearly a head shorter.

"Oh, but you should care. After you have walked the black sands of my realm and stood on the bank of my river. Granted, you did arrive there in a very unconventional way." Adam's chest sunk, and his mouth opened. How could this man know of his dream?

"No, it wasn't a dream," Mr. White said as if he could read his thoughts. "Although how you got there is a bit of a mystery. By the way, you really pissed off my boatman."

"Your boatman?"

"Yes, Jean. He takes his duties very seriously. No matter." Mr. White looked at the surrounding plants, at the brown dead crumpled leaves he had touched and the green he had not. He looked at Adam.

"Come here just a sec, would you?"

Adam took a small step backwards.

"Why?"

"Ah, indulge me, Adam. I'm curious. You are marked, correct? You sold your soul? What was it that you asked for?"

"I just want to grow things," Adam said quietly.

"Grow things? An odd request. Come. Touch this plant." He pointed at a shrivelled brown plant. Adam looked at it, then back to Mr. White.

"I don't understand."

"Just touch this plant for me. I'm curious. Come."

Adam stood, looking at Mr. White. Then he stepped forward and extended his hand. He paused and glanced back.

"What's going to happen?"

"Something wonderful," Mr. White whispered dramatically. He looked at Adam for a second, then he broke into a broad smile and chuckled. "I'm sorry. I love that line. Do you know it? It's from one of my favourite movies." He paused, "OK, not a movie fan. Come on, Adam. Touch the plant. We'll see together."

Adam's finger hovered inches from the dead plant.

"Touch it," Mr. White said.

Adam reached forward and touched the plant, then pulled his hand back quickly. Nothing happened. He watched the little brown leaf. He looked at Mr. White, a question in his eyes. He looked at the small brown plant. Nothing happened. Then, as he watched, the leaf shuddered and crumbled to dust. Adam's eyes widened. Almost immediately, a tiny little green shoot sprouted where the brown plant had been. It curved and spiralled up, getting greener and growing a small leaf. It looked like a time-lapse video. It continued to grow. A second leaf popped out, unwrapping itself and bending outward.

It grew a third, then a fourth leaf. It was now three times as tall as it had been. Adam leaned forward. He could hear the small wet noises as the plant grew, and he could smell the life there. Leaning even closer, his nostrils flared as he took a deep breath. The smell of life filled him. He swam in the experience of growth, of life but…there was another scent mixed in. Another part of the scent he thought of as 'life'. It was the opposite, it was death.

Adam opened his eyes and looked at Mr. White's smiling face.

"You see. We are like brothers, you and I. Well, maybe distant cousins."

Adam looked back at the plant.

"Cousins? I am not sure what you mean. Cousins?"

"No, I suppose not." Mr. White stepped to the glass wall and looked at the black-feathered mass in the grass.

"I needed that poor creature's sacrifice to come here. Its death is my duty. I have many names."

Adam looked at the dead crow. It was a crumpled mess, black against the green grass. He looked up at the glass pane the crow flew into. There was a star crack in the middle of the glass.

"What are you saying?" Adam asked, but he was alone in the greenhouse. He looked up and down the greenhouse. He walked deeper into the greenhouse, just in case. Mr. White was definitely not there. Adam started to wonder if Mr. White had been there. It felt like he had dreamt it. The more he thought about it, the more he was sure he had imagined it. Yes, it must have been a dream. He frowned. It was a dream, wasn't it? A dream?

He looked down at the dead, dry plants. The plants that had been alive, bright, green and full, until Mr. White touched them and took that brightness, took that life away.
Mr. White was Death.

Adam stared at the dry leaves, then walked a few steps and looked at the plant he touched. He stared at the delicate green leaves that he'd brought back. He touched the tip of one of the little leaves. It moved. It stretched and shivered as if a light breeze brushed past it. It curled up. Another new leaf pushed up. He pulled his hand back. And watched the now not so little plant.

Returning to the dead plants, he touched a dry leaf. It was like a small, thin sponge. It seemed to suck life from his finger. It puffed up and turned green, the green spread down the leaf, then the stalk. It straightened. The green spread out along till it was a fresh, bright plant. He touched another and watched it grow, renewed. Then another, then another, till all were back to green and alive.

He looked at what he had done. It felt good. He felt good. No, he felt great. He smiled. These were his plants. They filled him with joy. He closed his eyes and tipped his head back. He pulled in air, filling his lungs. The smell of earth and the green of life swirled within him. He felt it slip in, quiet and gentle. It slid up his chest and spread out his arms, and down his legs. He felt it fill him. His fingers tingled. His toes tingled. He stood for a long time, just letting himself feel, letting himself live.

When he looked down finally it was late afternoon. The sun was touching the treetops to the west. He didn't know how long he had stood there. A couple of hours, maybe. Not more surely. He walked down the aisle, touching each of the plants as he went. Feeling a small charge from each. When he got back to the end of the row, he turned and looked around. All the plants, all his plants, were waving as if in a gentle breeze.

He turned to leave and noticed the dead crow outside in the grass. One wing was tucked in tight, the other was spread out wide. Its head was turned awkwardly and lay on the outstretched wing. Its eyes were open. The black bead of the one eye reflected the darkening sky. He could feel something around it. He knelt and reached out a hand. He paused, not sure if he should, then touched the bird.

Immediately he felt energy leaving him, as if a faucet had been opened. It rushed out of him in a great gush. He stood dizzily. He felt nauseous. His eyes rolled white, he bent forward and vomited in the grass. Taking a breath, he sat back on his heels and looked about, confused. A wash of black passed over his eyes, and he tipped sideways. He didn't feel it when he hit the ground.

It was dark when he woke. He pushed himself into a sitting position. He felt frail and put his hand out to steady himself. The grass beneath his fingers was shrivelled, the circle around where he had lain, dead. He remembered the crow. It was gone, a dark patch of brown grass marked where it had been. The grass was brittle, almost as though it had been burnt. After a minute, he struggled to his feet. He was tired, so tired. He walked to the house, his house, he reminded himself. It didn't feel right, it felt like a fantasy or a dream that he would wake from.

Adam pushed open the large glass door to the kitchen. As it opened, he felt a shift in the air. When the door closed behind him, the house seemed to quiet. It hushed and stilled.

He needed a glass of water. He walked to the sink and picked up the glass that stood waiting for him, filled it from the tap and drank. As he finished, he realized what he had done. This was a new home. Why would there be a glass here just waiting for him? He looked at the glass. It was just like the glasses he had at his old apartment. He looked at it, confused. He opened the cupboard, it was full of dishes and cups, his dishes and cups.

Over the island, he looked into the front room. His couch and chairs looked shabby and tired in the clean space. He stared at the couch, swayed, and gripped the counter. He was too tired to think about it. He stumbled slightly as he walked to his couch and fell onto it. He was asleep in a second.

He didn't recognize what he was looking at. He was lying face down on his couch. His head turned to look out into the room. The angle was odd, but it didn't look like his apartment. The light was wrong. With his face pushed into his couch, he frowned. He closed his eyes; not yet awake, he could smell his couch. He had slept on it many times. It had a distinctive scent, a blend of foam, fabric, something sweet and feet.

He lay thinking he might go back to sleep, then he lifted his head and opened his eyes again. This wasn't his apartment. He wasn't sure what he was looking at. It was fuzzy. It was a red blotch against a neutral-coloured wall.

He blinked, and sat up, wiping the drool from his cheek and rubbed his eyes. When he opened them, they cleared, and he realized he was looking at a large dark red ceramic sculpture of a devil's head, complete with a huge white-toothed grin, pointed eyebrows and, of course, horns. He looked at it for a minute, then smiled. So Ol' Tom had a sense of humour.

Adam leaned back on his couch in 'His' living room and looked around. Everything that wasn't his, was carefully chosen. Mostly in a light oatmeal colour tastefully accented with black trim and small hits of black. The only exception was the red devil head that stood prominently against the curtains, now closed over the massive windows that looked out at the garden and his greenhouse.

"Coffee," he said to the empty, unfamiliar room. He stood and walked to the kitchen. He groaned with pleasure at seeing his coffee machine sitting in a corner. In a couple of minutes, he had a hot cup in his hand. He leaned at the island, looked at the house and took a sip. Once again, he reminded himself, this was his house.

Above him somewhere in the house, he heard an electric humming. He straightened, frowning, then the same humming started right behind him. He spun and saw a robot vacuum cleaner slide from under the kitchen cabinets. He watched for a minute, then he heard another start somewhere else in the house.

He smiled, "Cool, I always wanted one of those."

He had a friend that had one and was always bragging about it. He called it 'Rosey' after the robot maid on the Jetsons. Adam had always thought that was a pretentious idea. You don't name your toaster; why would you name your vacuum cleaner? No, there were at least three, maybe more robot vacuum cleaners in his house, and he wasn't about to name them.

He took his coffee, sat at the glass-top table in his breakfast nook, and admired his backyard. It was perfect. Everything was carefully thought out. The plants were curated for maximum effect, either for colour or shape or volume. It pleased him.

Then Rosey 1 stopped and started beeping. He finished his last sip of coffee and went over to it. Adam reached down, felt around for the release button and pulled the hopper out. He opened it and looked. It was full. In fact, it was stuffed with dead bits of flies. It was a horrible sight: black and glossy body parts mixed with legs and shiny thin wings. He emptied the hopper in the garbage, slid it back in, and pushed the button. Rosey 1 started to move again.

Above him, he heard Rosey 2 or maybe Rosey 3 beeping. He walked around the counter and headed upstairs. He found Rosey 2 in the middle of the hallway. It was stopped, and blinking red. He knelt and opened the hopper. She, too, was full of dead flies. Adam frowned. That was a lot of flies. He looked at the hopper. It was disgusting. Behind him, he heard Rosey 3 start to beep.

With the full hopper in his hand, he walked down the hall. Rosey 3 had stopped beeping. He opened a door where he thought he would find the robot. It was a bathroom, a really nice bathroom actually. It was the type of bathroom he had seen in magazines and online. With a smile he thought, he could get used to this.

He remembered the hopper in his hand. He turned and left the bathroom, crossed the hallway and opened the next door. It opened onto a large, beautiful room. It was set up as a den. His old oak desk sat in front of an oversized black leather chair. One wall was covered with a very simple bookcase. In front of the bookcase was a spectacular Eames recliner. He loved the look of them but never thought he would have one in his life.

"Yes, this is a bit of alright," he said to the room.

Rosey 3 was full of flies as well. Why so many flies? It made little sense. There were no flies at the windows or anywhere, the house was immaculate. He looked around, puzzled. With the two full hoppers in hand, he left the room and walked down the hallway.

At the top of the stairs, he surveyed the living room. His furniture looked small and tired in the grand space. Wait, when he had first arrived, hadn't there been a large flat leather couch here, not his tired old couch? The realization crept over him that, like his old couch and all his things, he didn't belong here. Really, who was he kidding? He hadn't won the lottery or anything. He just sold his downtown condo, and now here he was. He couldn't afford this, none of this. It was too much. Too perfect, too 'other'.

He looked at the fly-filled vacuum cleaner hoppers in his hands. Nothing made sense. How had his stuff got here? There was no way anyone could have moved his things in. He hadn't even packed. Had he sold his condo? He had signed no papers except for the representation agreement. This wasn't the way things worked.

"Excuse me, Mr. Gardner." The voice came from below. A man stood where the kitchen blended with the living room. He was dressed entirely in black with a large-brimmed hat. The man stood very straight, still and was smiling. He held a black book in front of him with both hands.

"Mr. September?" Adam asked as he walked down the stairs.

"No, my name is Mr. March."

"Mr. March? Why are you named after months?" Adam asked.

"Months? I'm not sure what you mean. My name is Mr. March."

Adam had reached the main floor. The strangeness of Mr. September at his condo and now this man, made Adam wary. He looked at Mr. March. His clothing was black, but it shimmered ever so slightly. He tried to look at the man's eyes but could not see them for the brim of his hat.

Adam walked past him and Mr. March followed, not turning his head but turning his body. A tingle ran up Adam's spine. The man rotated without stepping or moving his feet. He moved like he was on a turntable.

An edge of panic touching him, Adam continued to the garbage to empty the hoppers. When he turned back, Mr. March had his book open and was looking at something. He closed the book and said, "Ol' Tom would like to have a word." He raised his left arm, indicating the greenhouse.

Adam placed the empty hoppers on the countertop and looked out through the kitchen window at the backyard and the greenhouse. He turned back to Mr. March.

"He's waiting?" he asked, not sure why he was nervous.

After a moment, Mr. March said, "Yes."

Adam suddenly noticed Mr. March's legs were not separated. They were a solid single leg with shoes attached. He felt panic rising in him. The man that stood in front of him smiled and pointed out to the greenhouse. His mind swam, then Mr. March stepped forward, his legs separating as he stepped. Adam exhaled, relief flooding him. He had been mistaken; it was just a trick of the light.

"K," he said. He left the kitchen, and walked across the patio to the path that led to the greenhouse door. He glanced back at Mr. March. He was gone.

Adam opened the door and stepped into the moist, wonderful air. Ol' Tom stood with his back to Adam, looking at the plants which, Adam noticed, had grown significantly.

"So, it appears you had a visitor," Ol' Tom said, not turning around.

"A visitor?" Adam asked, confused, "You mean Mr. White?"

"Mr. White? Ha, yes, Mr. White. What a quaint name." Ol' Tom faced Adam smiling, "I'm sorry. How rude of me. How do you like your new home?"

"I can't afford this house. I can't afford any of this."

"Well, of course, you can. The deal is done. Signed, sealed and delivered."

"How can I afford this on my salary?"

Ol' Tom smiled in response, "Tell me about your visitor."

"My visitor? Oh, ya, that was kinda weird. He killed some of my plants," My plants? "Those plants," he pointed at the plants that now were nearly a foot high.

"They seem to be doing quite well," Ol' Tom casually said.

"Ya well, they weren't. He just touched them, and they died. They shrivelled and dried up."

"And you touched them and brought them back," Ol' Tom said.

"Ya." Adam stepped forward, pointing at the plants, his fingers outstretched as if reliving the moment when HE brought them back. He had done that. Hadn't he? He looked at the plants and smiled. Yes, he did.

Ol' Tom smiled and looked at his hands.

"This is a very odd situation we find ourselves in."

"I'm sorry. What are you talking about?" Adam asked.

"Well, let me clear it up for you. What you asked for…"

"What I asked for? All I wanted was to sell my condo and get a house with a garden," Adam said.

"Yes, but when we met, you asked for something quite different."

Adam thought back. The meeting had been a strange one. He realized he found it difficult to remember the details clearly. The meeting had taken on a feeling of a dream. He had walked and met Ol' Tom at the intersection at midnight. As he thought back, he was surprised at how calm he had been, how accepting. He had gone with very little protest, just said 'yes.'

"Ah, I see you are starting to get it." Ol' Tom said. "Anyway, you said, 'I want to grow life' but that is not right. Is it? You wanted something else, something more, didn't you?"

Suddenly there was a loud crack as a black crow smashed into the glass. Adam jumped and spun. The bird bounced off the glass almost in the same spot as the one last night. It landed on the grass, a mass of black feathers sticking out at odd angles.

"Not another crow," he said.

"Another crow?" Ol' Tom asked.

"Ya, last night when Mr. White was here, a crow hit the glass there." Adam pointed at the broken pane. Ol' Tom's gaze followed Adam's finger.

"Tell me, Adam, did the crow hit the glass before or after Mr. White arrived?"

Adam thought for a second, "Umm before, I think. Ya just before Mr. White arrived." Adam thought back, he was confused just how Mr. White had arrived.

"Yes, of course, after," Ol' Tom confirmed, "Mr. March, are you still here?"

"Yes sir," Mr. March said from behind Adam. Adam whirled, Mr. March's smile unnerved him.

"Mr. March, check on the house for Adam, and then your services are no longer required,"

Adam watched Mr. March walk away, back toward the house. He tried not to notice the odd way he walked. His steps had no effect on his upper body. He did not rise and fall with each step, just glided over his moving legs. It looked like the top half of his body had nothing to do with his lower half.

Adam wasn't sure what Mr. March was going to check, but it reminded him to ask about the house.

"About this house... How can I afford it?" he asked.

With a chuckle, Ol' Tom said, "Well, I see we are not going to have a visit from Mr. White after all."

Ol' Tom gestured out to the grass. The crow moved slightly, then, with an unsettling jerk, stood. It looked dazed, but it was alive.

Adam glanced toward the house. Through the glass, he

could see Mr. March standing like a statue in the middle of the kitchen, then, as if pushed, he fell forward. Surprised Adam turned to look at Ol' Tom, but he was no longer there. He ran from the greenhouse across the lawn and up the three steps to the door. It was open. He expected to see Mr. March sprawled on his floor, but he wasn't anywhere.

Adam was baffled. He couldn't figure out what had happened to Mr. March. The kitchen was littered with dead black flies. It was mesmerizing watching Rosey 1 go around the kitchen clearing the horrid mess.

He was lost in his own thoughts when he realized the crow had hopped into the kitchen and was watching him. Adam stood, knocking over the chair he had been sitting on. The crow, its feathers dirty and ruffled, shifted in jerky unsettling movements. It held its badly crushed head at a slight angle, looking at Adam with its remaining eye. Then its beak opened, and said, "You tall walker. You done dis. You done me a no good. Why'd ya do my self a no good? Ah, ask ya."

Adam's mouth fell open.

"Yes sir, yes sir, Ah plenty no good. Ah bin dun here, ya know? Bin dun ah dun, an yuz brung ma ground ways."

The crow leaped from the ground, its wings spread wide and attacked. Adam's arms flew up to protect his head. The crow flapped around him as it clawed and pecked, drawing blood from his arms. Adam flailed around as the crow attacked again and again. His fingertip happened to touch the crow's head, and there was a bright bluish flash. The crow was thrown backwards. It careened across the kitchen, smashed into the wall and flopped to the ground where it lay still.

Adam leaned against the kitchen cabinets breathing hard and watched as a small pool of black blood grew on the floor. The crow's body jerked, and its head came up, "Dun ma a no good tall walker. Kin't die no howz. Tis yer doin fer sure." it said as it struggled to stand.

Its right wing dragged on the floor as it stepped forward on one broken leg leaving a dribble of yellowy liquid. Its head tipped at a crazy angle.

"Kin't die no howz," it said, its single eye twisting wildly around till it found Adam.

"Yuz gat ah be fixen dis here poor shadow flyer. Jus wanna be in da dirt yes sir yes sir."

Rosey 1 snagged the crow's tail feathers. The crow squawked in surprise as it tugged, dragging the crow back and sideways. Adam looked around. Over the island hung his pots and pans. He grabbed his largest frypan. The crow squawked again, louder, trying to pull away from the grip of the vacuum. Adam raised the pan, hesitated, then slammed the heavy frypan down. There was a loud bang mixed with a muffled squawk and the crunch of bone. Rosey 1 bounced backwards, a couple of tail feathers stuck in its brush. It turned and moved off, dragging a smear of blackish blood and foul liquid. Adam lifted the pan and the crow squirmed, its eye rolling around frantically. It made a noise somewhere between a squawk and a groan.

He slammed the pan down again. The crow jerked; its one leg stuck out and pistoned madly. Adam panicked. He smashed the pan down again and again and again. When he lifted the pan this time, nothing was left that looked like a crow, just a shimmering mass of black jelly and broken feathers. Adam tossed the frypan in the sink. The black plastic handle was broken on one side. He looked down at the disgusting pile, "Fuck," he said, "What a mess."

He opened a tall thin cupboard that held a broom, and dustpan. He would need to mop, but first, he needed to get rid of what was left of the crow. He took the dustpan and a large

wad of paper towel and knelt down beside the mess. He wasn't
sure how he was going to go about this.

The black blood was spreading. After a couple of
aborted attempts, he finally pushed most of the mess into the
dustpan with the paper towel. He rose, trying hard not to look.
He was almost to the back door when he couldn't help himself
and glanced down. The black mass wriggled and squirmed,
sticky feathers turned. The shattered beak vibrated, trying to
open. What shocked him the most was the shiny bead that was
the crow's eye. Somehow still intact, it spun in the glistening
pile until it focused on Adam. Adam screamed and tossed the
dustpan and the horror it held away from himself.

It flew up to slap against the huge glass windows of
the kitchen. The dustpan fell to the floor with a clatter, but the
black writhing mass stuck high on the glass. It hung there for a
second, then slowly started to slide down leaving a black smear.
It sped up until it released entirely and hit the floor with a wet
splat. Adam looked at it lying there, a wriggling black pile of
feathers and jelly.

"Why aren't you dead?" he asked. He stepped closer.
Feathers coated in black made small jerking movements. The
smell was strong, decay and iron mixed with wet feathers and
something else he couldn't place. He went down on his knees
and brought his face close to the pile. As he got closer, it seemed
to squirm faster as if it were excited. Closer still, he drew in a
deep breath through his nose. He closed his eyes and tasted
the scents. It was fragrant with both death and life but there was
another scent, it was his own.

He opened his eyes, and he reached forward with his
right hand. He paused just before he touched the remains, then
he pushed his fingers deep into the mass. For a second, all he
felt was wet sticky warmth, then his nerves lit up. He pulled life

from the crow. He pulled at it, dragging that scent, his scent from it.

When he pulled his fingers out, they came smeared with black slime. He brought them to his nose. The scent was gone. Only the deep, dark scent of death was left. He grabbed some paper towel and wiped his fingers clean. He felt numb, removed. He pushed the mess back into the dustpan and walked out of the kitchen. He stepped down the wood steps that ended at a stone walkway surrounded by grass. On the last step, he felt his head swim, and he tripped. He fell straight forward, but he didn't land on grass. Instead, when he pushed up from where he had fallen, he was lying on cold black sand. It was dark. Far off, he could see the shape of distant mountains against the sky. He pushed himself up to a sitting position and, knowing where he was, looked around. To his left was the river; in front was the pier. A large boat like a massive gondola was moored at the end of the pier. Adam stood and brushed off his hands. He started walking towards the pier.

As he watched, the boat pushed off and slid quietly into the current of the river. He kept walking, all the while watching the boat move upstream. The boat looked small as it neared the far shore.

He looked back to the pier. A man stood at the end. Adam recognized the man's silhouette, it was Mr. White standing looking out across the river at the boat. When Adam stepped onto the planks, Mr. White turned and smiled. Adam looked at the handsome black man with the stacked hair and forked goatee. He was dressed as he had been.

"So you are Death," Adam said.

"I have so many names I do not know them all, but you knew that, Adam. You knew this place, and you knew who I was when I came to visit you."

"Ya, I suppose I did."

Mr. White smiled and looked out across the river.

"The boat is continuously making its runs. Jean is split between running his club and manning the oars."

"His club?" Adam asked.

"Yes, he runs several clubs for me." He turned and looked at Adam. "Let's go someplace a bit nicer."

White. Just white! Bright, brilliant white for a brief second, like the flash of a camera directly into his face. After the dark of the river valley, it blinded Adam and left spots that danced in front of his eyes. When the after images settled they found themselves standing in the greenhouse surrounded by the plants Adam had brought back to life.

"That's better," Mr. White said. Adam looked around, dazzled. He stepped back a step, his mouth open.

"So Ol' Tom gave you quite a gift." From the greenhouse, Mr. White noticed the black smear on the glass of the kitchen. "What did you do to my crow? I know she was on her way to me. She arrived, but then something changed. Now I see it was your doing."

"I didn't do anything to that bird. It attacked me," Adam said.

"Well. The crow was in my realm, and you dragged her back, at least a piece of her and not the nice part. I can't help wondering what Ol' Tom was thinking, giving you this 'gift'? It is not usual, I can tell you." Mr. White looked back at Adam, then he smiled. "I'm sorry, I was just thinking out loud. I know Ol' Tom has his reasons."

"Well, I think he was surprised I could do what I have been doing. I got the feeling he thought you had something to do with it," Adam said.

144

"Me? Now THAT is interesting." Mr. White seemed lost in thought.

Just for a second, Adam was sure he saw wings made of small bones and feathers attached to Mr. White's back drag against the planter boxes, as he walked deeper into the greenhouse. He stopped. Slightly embarrassed he said, "Sorry." He glanced over his shoulder, and the wings reappeared. They looked like a thousand small bones, maybe finger bones that had been laced together with thin strips of leather to form massive wings. Large black feathers were shoved here and there. Mr. White looked at Adam with a weirdly shy pride and stretched his wings out. They creaked, leather and bone straining. They were very impressive but could not open completely in the confines of the room. They scraped against both glass walls.

"Wow!" Adam breathed. Mr. White beamed. He was obviously very proud of his wings, "I don't usually unfold them. They were a gift." He smiled with pleasure as Adam looked at them.

"A gift? That's an unusual gift."

"Yes. Honestly, you do not know the half of it," Mr. White said, a hardness in his voice.

Adam looked at him, not understanding.

"The wings were given to me by someone I held very dear." Mr. White seemed to regret saying anything. "I must be off. I will visit you soon."

Adam stared at the spot where Mr. White had stood. Adam hadn't liked Mr. White's last words. Did I mean that I would die soon, or did he mean simply that he was going to visit again?

Adam walked down the greenhouse looking at his plants. The plants he had 'revived' were huge, far larger than the plants he hadn't touched, but their shape was disturbing. They were twisted and gnarled, hideous versions of what they had been. As he studied them, they seemed to sense him, and moved toward him. He was shocked to realize he felt fear. There was anger in these plants, anger towards him. He stepped back. He left the greenhouse and went to the kitchen.

The black smear on the glass was gone. Someone or something had cleaned the mess up. He looked, not understanding. It was only early afternoon, but he was exhausted. He felt as though he could barely stay upright. He walked into the living room and sat on his couch, planning to just sit for a minute or two.

It was dark when he woke though he wasn't sure what time it was. He had stretched out on the couch at some point. The clock on the stove read 3:36. He had slept for several hours, and yet he still felt tired. He walked up to his bedroom not questioning the house or any of the strangeness around him.

He would have to call Jerry in the morning. He wasn't sure what he'd say. He wasn't going to work anytime soon. How was he going to explain this to him, or for that matter, anyone? It didn't make sense. It didn't even make sense to him if he stopped to think about it. He was too tired to worry about it. As he undressed and lay down on the bed, he hoped he wouldn't dream. He hoped Death, and the Devil, would leave him alone just for tonight.

The black water was nearly up to his knees, and swirled around his legs. It moved like something alive. He watched it as it curled, little fingers of black reaching up his legs.

Panicked, he leaped back onto the cool black sand; his heart beat frantically. He felt slightly dizzy, his breath came in short, ragged gulps. His legs were completely dry. The water slid from him, twisting its way back to the river, small snakes of inky black that curled and wriggled. He watched them till they had slithered completely back into the river. The river seemed to tug at him gently, urging him to walk into its swirling blackness. It took an effort to turn from its undulating surface and walk away from its call.

As soon as he looked away, the river's call weakened. His breathing slowed. His heart returned to normal. He felt something was wrong even though he couldn't point to what it was. He knew where he was, but it felt different. As before the far-off mountains stood, massive black shapes against a dark sky. He couldn't decide how far away they were. They seemed a long way, but at the same time, very close. The black sand beach was empty for as far as he could see. The air was very still and cool, almost cold.

He trudged up the bank, putting a bit of distance between the river and himself. He had no destination, just felt he needed to move, not to stand still. It was definitely colder, not cold enough to see his breath if that were possible here, but cold. As he walked, he felt a light breeze from behind him.

Far off on the beach, he saw a movement, a flicker. It vanished, but he was sure he had seen something. He squinted, straining to see. He kept walking, staring hard at the spot. Yes, there it was again. He started walking faster. The light breeze seemed stronger, almost pushing him forward. There was definitely movement. He was walking fast now, nearly running. The movement disappeared. He slowed. The breeze that had been sporadic was now constant. No longer a breeze, but a wind. The black sand shifted, kicked up as he walked. Something about the wind made him uneasy.

The movement was back, it was a figure waving its arms. Adam was unsure if the figure was waving in greeting or trying to warn him. Each step he took kicked up more sand. The wind caught the grains and carried them forward. It was definitely a man waving with both arms. There was something familiar about him. He was definitely trying to warn him.

He glanced behind him. He could no longer see those distant mountains. They were completely obliterated by the darkness. Flying sand stung his face. He squinted into the wind. Swirls of sand slid past him. He looked back at the man. He was frantically waving both arms high in the air. Adam started to run. The wind pushed at his back. He could hear an indistinct mumbling on the wind. The man seemed to be getting more frantic. Adam ran faster. The wind now was a force against his back, threatening to push him over.

With a sudden jolt, he realized that he recognized the figure. It was himself. He skidded to a stop. He watched himself wave wildly and point past him. The figure started to run towards him.

The wind surged. Tendrils of black sand wrapped around him and grabbed him. They closed around his body like massive fingers, and squeezed. He was lifted off the ground. The 'other Adam' was screaming as he ran forward. Adam couldn't hear the words, just saw the wide-open mouth. There was terror on his face.

Suddenly Mr. White was beside Adam. "Time to go," he said as he slid his arm around Adam's waist and pulled. Adam had a glimpse of himself standing on the black beach, arms raised, a defeated look on his face, then he was standing in his new kitchen with Mr. White. Adam staggered slightly, and caught himself on the edge of the counter.

Mr white smiled. "Well, that was interesting. How are you doing, Adam?"

"I'm fine," he said without thinking. Of course, he wasn't

fine. He was shaking. It had felt like a giant hand had grasped him and squeezed.

"Good. Well, I'll stop by in a couple of days. Have a great day," Mr. White walked into the air.

Adam opened his mouth, but it was too late to say anything. The kitchen was immaculate; every surface was perfectly cleaned and polished.

He looked at the clock; 10 in the morning. He felt tired. He always felt tired. He never used to feel tired. Now he felt it all the time. If he was awake, he felt tired.

He moved about the kitchen on autopilot, making coffee. He walked into the living room with a mug in his hand and sat. He thought about the black beach and the 'other him' standing there in his dream.

"It was a dream," he said out loud to the empty room. It sounded false. "It was a dream," he whispered, unsure.

His thoughts were interrupted by a banging on the door. It was Jerry, his boss and he looked upset. Adam rose and walked to the door, "Jerry?" Adam said. "Come in."

"Adam. You look like shit. What the hell is going on? I went to your apartment. The door was wide open, and it looked like it had been ransacked. There was shit scattered about. It was an absolute mess. It took me a couple of days to find out where you had moved to. I thought you were faking being sick. Thought you'd inherited some money," Jerry paused, "but you are sick, aren't you?"

"I'm fine," Adam said, not really knowing what to say.

"Fine?" Jerry said. "Have you looked at yourself? You are not fine. You look like shit. You've lost a ton of weight."

Adam looked down. Yes it was true, he had noticed, but ignored it. Losing weight was a good thing, wasn't it? But it was more than that. He felt drained all the time. Even now, as he stood, he was feeling faint.

"Come in, Jerry," Adam said, and without waiting he turned, walked to the front room and sat, grateful to have made it to the couch. Jerry followed but didn't sit.

"Adam. You don't look good," he said quietly, "and what's with this house? Whose is it?"

"It's mine," Adam said. He looked down, suddenly embarrassed, "It's mine."

"Yours? I don't understand. Yours? How can it be yours? Did you come into some money?"

"No, I just have a very good realtor." Adam stood. "Jerry, why are you here?"

"Why am I here?" Jerry looked stunned, "you don't show up for work for weeks. Your apartment looks like you were robbed, and you look like you are deathly sick. I'm worried about you."

Adam looked at Jerry. Tears rose in his eyes. Adam was touched. They never really had hung out. They worked together and after so many years seeing each other every day, they had become friends.

Adam stepped forward and wrapped his arms around Jerry. He was crying. He hugged Jerry.

"Thank you, Jerry. I hadn't realized how much I needed someone to care. I have been in a very strange situation for the last few weeks. You would not believe me if I told you all that has happened."

Jerry hugged him back hesitantly. Hugging wasn't something he did, but he did now.

"It's OK," Jerry said.

Adam couldn't believe how good it felt to hug someone. He hadn't known how badly he'd needed it. He squeezed a bit harder, and something shifted. He hugged Jerry tightly and started to feel better for it. He felt his body regain its energy. He felt strength come back into his arms. He groaned as vitality swam through him. He felt the pounding of his blood in his temples. He squeezed harder, pulling Jerry into him. He released Jerry, feeling embarrassed at hugging so hard and for so long. He pulled away, mumbling an apology.

Jerry stood swaying in front of him. All colour had left him. He had shrunk. His eyes stared out of dark holes in his sagging face. He looks like a balloon that lost its air, Adam thought, even as he felt the horror of what he was seeing. Jerry's clothes hung off him in large drapes. His pants slid to the floor. Adam watched them pool on the floor around Jerry's shoes. When he looked back up, Jerry's face looked grey and cracked. It started to flake like burnt paper. Jerry's eyes opened wider, his irises turned milky and he crumpled to the ground. Adam stood looking down at the pile of clothes covered in what looked like ashes. Adam sat heavily on the floor.

"Finally!" a voice said from behind Adam. He leaped to his feet. Mr. White was standing behind him, smiling and lightly clapping.

"It took you a while, but you finally got there," Mr. White said.

"What...what do you mean?" Adam asked.

"Ha. Look at yourself. I thought the next time I came here was going to be for you. But no. It's for your poor friend here." Mr. White gestured to the pile of clothes. Adam looked at the clothes, feeling confused.

"I don't know what happened to him. He just fell apart," Adam said.

"You did that. That's all you."

"I didn't do that!"

"No? Are you sure? Felt pretty good to suck the life out of him, didn't it?" Mr. White smiled at Adam.

Adam frowned, "I didn't do anything." Adam knew he had even as he said it.

"Haven't you noticed when you give life to your plants or to that poor crow that other day, you get weaker?" Mr. White asked.

Adam didn't say anything.

"Well, no matter. Now that you know, what are you going to do about it?"

Adam looked back at Jerry's remains. When he looked back, Mr. White was gone.

Adam cursed softly. He thought about all that had happened in the last few weeks. It all felt dreamlike. He had no good rationale for any of it.

He headed for the greenhouse. He pulled the glass door open and caught his reflection. It stopped him. He looked at himself. It was him, but like he had never seen himself ever in his life, not even in his teens. The person reflected in the glass was beautiful. He was straight, strong and muscular. He looked down at himself. His arms were ribbed with muscle, with meaty biceps, heavy triceps and nearly heroic forearms and chest. He had a body like Jean Claude. He looked back up to his reflection and grinned.

Now this was great, he thought and smiled.

He continued to the greenhouse, a new spring in his step. In the greenhouse, he smiled at the pleasure as he breathed in the wonderful moist, rich musk of the growing plants. He closed his eyes and breathed. He opened his eyes and looked down the rows at his plants. Adam smiled at the health and vitality he saw there, the shades of green busting with life, until he saw the few plants he had brought back to life. Those burst with life but not the life he recognized. If it was 'life' it was a dark life, almost an anti-life.

The plants they had started out to be were twisted. They had grown massive sprouting great tentacles that had reached out, strangling the smaller plants that shrivelled and turned black. The grotesque plants brandished black flowers with stamens that dripped a dark syrup.

Adam pulled back from them. With rising horror, he realized they shifted slightly, reacting to his presence.

These abominations were killing his plants. He ran back to the kitchen and grabbed the biggest chef knife he had. Armed, he attacked them. He hacked at their stalks, cleaving through even as they slowly reached for him. One black blossom spat at him, hitting his shoulder with its dark liquid. It burned like acid where it touched Adam's skin. Gritting his teeth he kept hacking. A chemical smell filled the air. The acid burned his arm. It started to go numb. A weird tingle began spreading from the burnt spot outward. When he realized he could no longer swing the knife with that arm, he switched hands and continued until he had hacked them all to pieces.

He stood gasping for breath. His right arm was nearly useless, hanging limply at his side. He was covered in black gore and sap. He staggered back, staring at the destruction he had wrought. He stumbled to the door. He needed to get to the house. He didn't make it. He had just stepped through the greenhouse door when a wave of darkness clamped down on his head, and he fell forward. He did not feel himself hit the ground.

Immediately he knew where he was. The black sand stretched out in front of him. He started walking, looking for his 'other' self. He had questions, and he didn't know how long he had.

After a few paces, he broke into a run. Far down the beach, he could see a brighter spot. He hoped it was him.

As he ran, he called his own name. The lighter spot grew and became a figure seated on the sand, looking out on the river. He called louder. The figure didn't seem to hear him.

Behind Adam, a breeze began to push against him. He ran faster, calling out, but there was no reaction from the figure. When he was close enough to see it was him, he slowed. There was something not right. The figure was very still.

The breeze buffeted him. He picked up his pace, running flat out. He slid to a stop only a few paces from the seated figure. The figure that sat there was himself dressed in a white shirt and light coloured pants. He sat with his arms wrapped around his knees. He must have died that way. He was nearly a skeleton. What flesh remained was shrivelled and dried like leather.

Adam walked up to the corpse. How long had he sat here? How long had Adam been away? Wasn't it just a few hours ago? He stood looking down at the man that had been, while the breeze built, tugging at him. Adam took a step back as the corpse's head turned, creaking like old leather, and regarded him with shriveled raisin-like eyes.

"So, you finally returned," it said, jaw creaking. It began to move with jerking hesitant movements. With a sound like breaking twigs mixed with tearing cloth, it rose up onto its feet and turned to Adam.

The white shirt and pants started to tear with the movement, exposing the brittle grey-brown flesh and bone beneath. Fabric tore, and bits dropped as it raised its arm, reaching for Adam.

"I didn't think you would come back. I thought the temptation had been too great."

"Temptation?" Adam asked.

"Yes, to play God."

"God? What do you mean?"

More bits of cloth tore and fell. Bits of dry, leathery flesh broke off, dropping to the black sand. The breeze was now a wind that pulled at them both.

"Look! We don't have much time, and it's too late to undo it. Think about what we asked for from Ol' Tom, what we have always wanted."

"I just wanted a garden to grow things," Adam said.

"Fuck, I can be so stupid. Think about what you really wanted. I won't be here next time you stop by. Time is very different here. I know you know because I am you, but you have to say it. I am only your shade. The soul you sold to Ol' Tom."

The wind now was howling. The corpse that was Adam could barely stand against the constant buffeting. The white shirt was now just a few strips of fabric strung across the ribs and arms of the dead Adam.

As Adam watched, the arm that was extended towards him broke off and fell to the ground. Both Adams watched it fall.

"Again?" a voice said, just audible above the wind. "You are tenacious," Mr. White said as he grabbed Adam by the shoulders and shoved him.

Adam opened his right eye. He was lying on his lawn. The sun was up. He had no idea how long he had lain in the grass, one leg still half in the greenhouse.

In front of his eye, he could see blades of grass. As he had as a child, he watched fascinated as a small black beetle walked up a blade of grass. It reached the top, which had been cut off by a lawnmower and was square with a brown edge. The beetle perched for a second on the pinnacle, rocked, then spread its elytra, and large filmy wings unfolded. Adam was pleased he still remembered the proper name of the parts of a beetle.

He was tempted to catch the small creature and take it inside to examine it as he had so many times before; however, this time, he watched it leap, dip slightly, then fly away.

He lay for a few minutes more. He pushed himself up on all fours, then stood. His right arm was shrunken. Its skin was thin and papery, like the arm of a very old man. He flexed his fingers. The bones stood out under the pale skin. He compared his left hand to his right. His left was full and youthful, as was the rest of his body. His clothes were both burnt looking and crusted with dried greenish spots. His t-shirt and his jeans were full of holes, and they smelled horrible.

Adam looked back at the plants, his plants. The plants he had attacked were blackish brown, a thin smoke curled from them. All the smaller plants around them were dead, drooping down and turning brown, but the plants further away looked OK.

He went to the house to change.

In his bedroom, he pulled off his ruined clothing and tossed them on the floor. He examined his reflection in the full mirror. He was quite a sight. Most of his body was untouched by the poison except for a few burnt spots. His right arm hung nearly skeletal at his side, a stark contrast to his left arm which was bursting with health. He had never looked like this. He had abs! He was beautiful, a perfect example of a gymnast or professional swimmer. He admired the vision of himself in the mirror.

He smiled as he thought, I look like a Greek god.

The doorbell rang.

Adam turned from the mirror and took some clothes from the closet. He pulled on a pair of pants and put on a shirt as he left the bedroom and walked downstairs. He finished buttoning the last button when he noticed he had put on a fine white linen shirt and a quick glance down confirmed he had on light coloured pants.

As he walked across the front room, he saw a small shape standing at his door. He opened the door and looked at the young girl standing there holding a box of cookies, a Girl Guide in full uniform, a bag beside her with more boxes of cookies.

"Hi, my name is Melissa, and I am selling Chocolatey Mint Cookies to raise funds for our annual trip to the museum. By buying boxes of Girl Guide cookies, you'll be helping us reach our goals. Each box of Girl Guide cookies is only $5, and every box brings us closer to our museum trip," she said, sounding bored.

For a second, Adam just stared. This normal event seemed so out of place in his life. It made everything that had happened even stranger, more bizarre.

"Humm? Yes, Yes, of course, I'll buy 4. Just give me a second to find my wallet," he said, and walked away leaving the door open.

Melissa stepped into the house, set her bag down and started pulling out boxes. She was smiling, happy to be selling the last of her cookies.

Adam returned, pulling a twenty from his wallet and extending it to her. She took it, slipped it into her pocket and picked up the boxes of cookies. Adam reached for the cookies, and the fingers on his right hand touched Melissa's hand.

Immediately he could feel warmth and strength flow into his fingertips. He grasped her hand and pulled. She yelped and dropped the boxes of cookies. Adam held her hand and watched it shrink as his arm puffed up like a balloon. He gripped her tighter as she struggled. The flow of strength and energy sped up. He could feel it flow into him like a hose, up his arm and into his body.

It felt amazing. He closed his eyes when he noticed she had stopped struggling. Her eyes bulged. Her face sank into itself. He opened his eyes when he could no longer feel her hand in his. Beside the boxes of cookies and the bag was the uniform in a pile scattered with white ashes.

He stood looking at the pile, horrified by what he had done. He staggered backward till he was against the couch. He sat still, staring at the pile.

"Well, I never saw this coming. A Girl Guide," Mr. White stood beside Adam, "That's some 'godly' shit right there."

Adam looked up at Mr. White.

"What?" Adam said.

"It's the sort of thing a god would do, don't you think? I mean killing off an innocent just to gain more life," Mr. White said.

Adam looked at him. He remembered the word he had said to himself on the black beach, "...to play god," he whispered.

"Yes! Now You are getting it. Ol' Tom certainly has a sense of humour. Twisted for sure." Mr. White chuckled.

"I don't understand," Adam said, looking at Mr. White, "All I wanted was a house with a garden to grow things."

"Fuck, you are slow. Your shade was so right about you, which I guess makes sense. He is you." Mr. White reached into his jacket and pulled out a bright object and set it down in front of Adam, "He also said you would be needing this."

Adam looked at the handgun that gleamed on the table. He frowned and looked back at Mr. White. His eyes returned to the gun, then to the small pathetic uniform in a pile surrounded by scattered cookies.

He had killed her, taken her life and brought it into himself. He glanced at his right arm, no longer shrunken, now full, strong and youthful.

He knew he had felt amazing as he did it, as the energy had flowed into him, but he also knew that it was the power he felt over her that had felt good. He had the power of life and death just as he had over his plants and over that bug in the yard. It wasn't life he loved and wanted. He knew that when he had met Ol' Tom what he had asked for was the power of life AND death. He wanted that power, the power of both life and death. He wanted the power of a god.

Mr. White smiled, "There you go. You've got it."

Adam knew it was true. The knowledge rocked him. How he had defined himself for his entire life as a nice, caring man. Now that was flipped upside down. He saw himself in a new dark light. A light he did not like.

He could live forever, knowing he was not the man he had thought he was. Or he could stop now. Even as he thought it, he knew his decision. It had been there all along. His decision had been sitting on the banks of the black river waiting.

The temptation of forever was great, but it's impossible to live forever when you can't live with yourself, even for a minute longer.

Adam reached for the chrome weight that sat on the table in front of him. He turned the surprisingly small black hole towards himself, positioned his thumb over the trigger, opened his mouth and slid the cold barrel in. It clicked against his teeth, hard and cold.

A line came to him, remembered from long ago, "Sometimes the only solution is a lead pill."

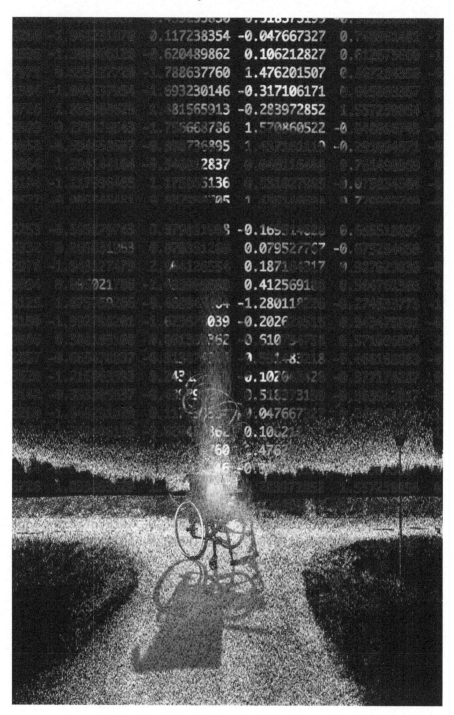

# CHAPTER 7

## ADDING IT UP

Simon wasn't happy. He hadn't been happy for a while, if ever. He was a list maker, and the list he had made of all the things that made him happy was short, very short. The truth: nothing really made him happy except his lists and perfect numbers. Happy wasn't the right word; less unhappy would be more accurate.

Simon was a middle school math teacher. His awkward, somewhat shy nature did not interfere with his teaching, and he was an excellent teacher.

He made lists of everything he could, even attempting to list his lists. Some people collected stamps or coins. Simon had tried these and found making the list of the coins or stamps and counting them far more satisfying than the collection itself.

Simon dreamt of two things, the two things that would make him less unhappy. The first was a perfect number that no one else had. The second was a list he could compile, a list that would be his, and only his, a list that had never existed before and probably would never exist again. He just didn't know what that list or that number might be.

Late on a Tuesday night at a truck stop just outside of town, he found a glimmer of what his list might be. He was sitting having a coffee. It was late...or rather, early. He went for drives when sleep eluded him, which it did most nights. Never deciding where he would go, he would just follow whatever whim presented itself to his mind. Often the following day, he would not remember where he had driven or for how long.

That night he had driven for several hours when his gas gauge showed he was low. He pulled into an all-night truck stop to fill up. He rolled up to the pumps and stopped. There was no one else filling up.

He got out of his car and looked around. The night was clear, stars overhead, and the highway was almost empty, only the occasional rig breaking the darkness.

He stood, hand on the filler nozzle, looking down at the ground. A cab-over semi pulled off the highway into the parking lot. After it hissed to a stop, a man stepped down.

Simon watched him crunch across the gravel parking lot to the old-style diner with a large window and DINER written in large letters above it. Simon could see the man as he sat at the stools and spoke to the waitress.

The nozzle clicked. Simon replaced it and closed his filler cap, still looking at the activity in the diner. After a minute, the waitress left and returned with something she placed in front of the trucker. Simon couldn't tell what it was from this distance.

Back in his car, he watched the diner. He had bought this piece of shit from Carson Ford a few months back and had hated the car right from day one. One headlight had burnt out the week he had brought it home. He could not complain, not that he would have had the courage to. Johnny Carson had died in an animal attack. The attack was still in the news, and the talk around town, nine dead bodies and two others missing. It had been a good day for numbers, but now the dealership was closed. Simon was stuck with his personal POS.

He looked at the trucker talking to the waitress. Without deciding to, he drove up to the front of the diner and parked.

He got out of his POS and went into the brightly lit greasy spoon. The waitress looked up, smiled and gestured around the room with a 'Sit anywhere' sweep of her arm.

The trucker had a coffee and a slice of pie in front of him. Simon wondered what kind of pie it was.

Through a pass-through, Simon saw a thin, grey-skinned man with a ball cap and stained apron, squinting over a steaming flattop. Simon walked past the trucker to a booth at the very end of the room, near the window, and slid in.

The waitress was beside him in a second, "Coffee?" she said with a practiced smile. She was carrying a full glass pot.

"Sure...yes. Um, what kind of pie do you have?" He looked up and attempted a friendly smile. He was only half successful. After a pause, she looked back to the counter where a glass case held a rotating display with slices on plates. She already knew what was there, but it was a gesture she did out of habit. She looked back at Simon and said, "Well, we have apple, cherry, and a fresh rhubarb and apple. That's the best."

"Then that's what I'll have. Sounds delicious. Thanks,"

"Ok, Hun." She flipped over a cup in front of Simon and, with an expert hand, splashed coffee into the cup without spilling a drop, left and returned in a minute with a slice of rhubarb and apple pie.

"Anything else?" she smiled.

"No, thank you. This is great."

"Ok, Hun." She hustled back to her perch at the end of the counter.

Simon took a sip of the coffee. It was good, but very hot. He never liked coffee too hot. He picked up his fork and glanced up at the waitress. She had pulled out a paperback and was reading, looking up every so often to see if her two customers needed anything.

The waitress was right. The pie was fresh and delicious. Simon had just enjoyed the last bite, when two bikes pulled up to the window right beside him, the rumbling making him flinch. Simon watched the two men shut the bikes down and tip them over onto their kickstands. They stood and looked back to the pumps. Simon followed their gaze. Two more bikes were there, filling up.

The two bikers stood for a minute. After a word, they walked to the door of the diner. As soon as they entered, the air changed. The waitress leaped to her feet, dropping her book, and rushed to walk them to a booth. The trucker dropped some money on the counter and left.

Simon watched them walk, tall and thin, in leather and denim, behind the waitress. Each had a denim vest over his jacket.

The waitress sat them in a booth, one over from where Simon sat watching. He heard her talking. Her voice was brighter than he had heard.

"I'm Sheri. What can I get you?" she beamed.

The biker closest to the window waved to his friends that were still at the pumps. The other smiled at the waitress and said, "Just coffee," She smiled back and poured two coffees.

"Two more," the biker who had been waving said as he settled in his seat, his leather jacket creaking.

Simon sipped his coffee. It was at the perfect temperature. Inside, he smiled. Beside him, the other two bikes rolled up and parked. The two men walked into the diner. The first lifted his chin in a quick greeting and walked to the booth. They each glanced at Simon, turned and slid into the booth opposite their friends. They dressed the same.

On the back of the vests was a crest. It read "The Jurors" in an arc on the top and "666 deal" on the bottom. Simon had seen the crest before. Everyone in the area had. They were a bike club with a clubhouse west of here. They seemed to be more interested in building bikes than anything, although rumours said they were into something else. That 'something else' was never stipulated.

Four bikers. Four bikes. Simon counted. He chuckled. He felt like the Count.

The bikers were laughing about something. One turned and looked at Simon.

"Hey, man. What kind of pie did you have?"

"Ah...Rhubarb and apple." Simon stuttered.

"Good?"

"Ah...yes, very," Simon sort of smiled.

"Thanks," the biker said and turned back, raising a finger to the waitress who hurried over, took the order and returned with a piece of pie. She hesitated, waiting for more orders. She returned to her perch, disappointed. And did not pick up her book, just sat waiting.

Simon watched the bikers talking. They seemed tired.

Maybe they had been riding for a while. They had that road-weary look. They spoke in low tones, not looking at each other. Their laughter when it came was subdued.

Simon watched them, wondering what it was like to be them, what it was like to live as they did. They were so different from him. Their lives were nothing like his ordered life. He imagined the chaos that was their lives. Freedom, they would call it, outside of society, one-percenters. He imagined himself on a bike roaring down the road. No one was waiting for them. No job, no boss yelling, no numbers, no lists.

He stopped: no lists? Did he really not want lists? How could that be? They had been the driving force of his entire life. He looked at his half-empty coffee, then finished it with a swallow. He looked up as the waitress stopped beside his table, "Top'er up?" she said with a smile as she peered over her shoulder at the bikers.

"Sure...Yes," he said.

She turned back, "I'm sorry...yes, ok." She refilled his cup and walked away, passing slowly by the biker's booth.

Simon watched the dark road through the window. It was quiet; no trucks passed, no cars, just the dark. Staring out the window, his focus shifted. He saw his own reflection. A small man, narrow shoulders, scruffy beard that did not cover his small chin. "Weak chin." Isn't that what they called it. Weak. Is that what he was? Weak?

He was pulled from his thoughts by a loud bike pulling up to the diner. Simon looked out as the rider shut down. The man that stood was tall, like the others, but he was different. He had a long black beard. He was dressed as the others, jeans and a black leather jacket with a denim vest and the same patch on his back, but where they all walked with a swagger, he moved as a wolf might, smooth, unhurried. Where they wore bravado in their smiles, his solemn visage radiated calm readiness. He walked in, and the bikers went quiet.

"Jacob," one biker said, standing. Jacob waved him back down. He glanced at Simon, then back at the bikers.

"So?" he asked. His voice was deep. He looked at the four sitting drinking coffee, "How's the pie?" His face broke into a smile. It did not touch his eyes.

The waitress brought a chair to the booth. Jacob glanced at the waitress who shied away from him. He took the chair and sat. The second he walked in, he owned the room.

"Oh," he touched her hand, then asked the biker with a plate with pie crumbs, "What kind of pie did you have?"

Before the biker could answer, the waitress blurted, "rhubarb and apple." She bit her lip.

Jacob considered the waitress, "Then that's what I will have...and a coffee." He smiled at her, then looked back at the bikers.

She moved away, quickly returning with a piece of pie. She poured a coffee and left, just as quickly.

Jacob took a bite of pie, smiled, and took another. He put his fork down and took a sip of coffee.

"This is good," he said, "very good." Jacob looked to the waitress and waved her over. She came, launching herself off her stool to go to his side.

"You bin here a while?" Jacob asked.

Simon watched the waitress. She looked like a rabbit caught in the headlights of an oncoming truck. She stood blinking at Jacob.

"Couple years," she said.

"Who owns this joint?" Jacob lifted the cup of coffee. She looked down at the coffee.

"You want a refill?" Her voice broke.

"No darlin'. What's this place called?" He put his coffee down on the table.

The waitress looked at the surrounding bikers, "The Scratching Post?" Her voice was small.

Jacob looked at her and smiled, "Of course it is. Thank you."

The waitress scurried away.

"Yup, that makes sense," Jacob said as he took another sip of coffee, "it's that good." He took another fork of pie and smiled. "Fucking Frank. It's his deal."

Simon sipped his coffee, not understanding what the 'deal' was but loving the coffee.

"Who are you?" Jacob asked, suddenly standing beside Simon's table, coffee in his hand. Simon hadn't noticed him move toward him. Jacob slid into the booth opposite Simon.

"I'm sorry?" Simon stumbled.

"Don't be sorry. I jus' wanna know who you are," Jacob said.

"My name is Simon," Simon said.

"Simon. Ok, Simon, why are you here?" Jacob took a swallow of coffee.

"I'm just having a coffee."

"Yes, I can see that, and it's excellent coffee, but it's very late. It's not usual for someone like yourself to be out this late." Simon looked into Jacob's eyes. They were grey with a touch of blue ice over a frozen lake. As he looked, something crossed those eyes. He saw something he hadn't seen before. He thought for a second, "I can't sleep."

"That's the worst, ain't it, but that doesn't answer my question now, does it?"

"I can't sleep, so I go for drives. It calms me," he said.

Jacob nodded, "Ok, well, me and my friends here are going to have a little meeting. Kinda need a bit ah privacy."

"Oh...Ya...Ok," Simon said. He slid sideways, "I'll just pay my bill."

"I'll get that. It's the least I kin do fer disturbin' your late-night feedin'."

Simon smiled, feeling grateful for no real reason, "Thank you."

They stood awkwardly, ending up facing each other. Jacob was more than a head taller. Simon shuffled around the much bigger man and walked past the booth of watching bikers. He noticed the waitress and the cook were nowhere to be seen. As Simon stepped into the night air, four more bikes slowed on the highway and pulled into the diner's lot.

Simon unlocked his car and climbed in as the bikes pulled up beside him. He waited till they shut down and walked past him, then backed out. Out of the corner of his eye, he watched the new group join the group in the diner with hugs and backslaps. Nine bikers, all with the same patch on their back. 'The Jurors.'

Driving forward, he turned toward the pumps, his one headlight glinting off the chrome of the lined-up bikes. He pulled past the pumps, then he stopped. He could just roll out onto the blacktop and head home and continue with his life. Nothing would change, and his diner stop would be forgotten in the morass that was his life. But what if...?

He turned the car away from the highway. He made a big circle and stopped beside a large trailer that had been parked as far from the pumps and diner as the lot would allow. Simon backed up beside it until his car was in its shadow. He shut the car off, sat and waited.

From here, he could see the diner's large front window.

He could see movement, but not much detail. He sat watching the restaurant.

After a half-hour, four more bikes rolled in. Thirteen bikers in a diner. A weird Doctor Seuss book. He watched with no actual plan other than to observe and decide what to do when they left. Maybe follow them or something.

He woke stiff but more rested than he had felt for weeks. The sun was up. There were a couple of vehicles parked in front of the diner, but no bikes. He started his car and pulled up to the diner, and went in. A different waitress showed him to the same booth he had been in earlier.

Twelve people, including the cook and waitress.

He slid into the booth as the waitress poured a coffee he hadn't asked for. She placed a large, plasticized menu in front of him, went to the next booth and refilled their cups. She returned and stood over him, hand on her hip holding a small pad and pen, the other holding the coffee pot in the air.

"Umm... couple of eggs over easy and bacon?"

"You want toast?"

"Yes, please." He handed her back the menu. She took it and left without another word.

He sipped his coffee. Still too hot, but delicious. He looked around the diner. It was a different room, with people laughing, moving about, and eating.

He thought back to the night before and the bikers and their late-night meeting. What had that been about? They seemed to have come from different directions. Who are the Jurors? Who is Jacob?

The waitress brought Simon his breakfast. He ate, thinking about the bikers until the food broke through his thoughts.

"My god, this is good," he said between mouthfuls.

When he finished, he felt a sense of loss, looking at his empty plate.

He glanced at his watch. Almost 10? How could it be?

He rose, paid his bill, left the diner and headed home. On the way, he stopped at a small corner store to buy his weekly lotto ticket. He always played the same number. It was messy, not clean like he would prefer, but it was a prime number, and that was the purest number he could find. His number was 790879.

It was Saturday, so there was a stack of things he should do. There was always marking to be finished. He shuffled around his apartment, moving from one thing to the next, unable to settle. He felt restless, unfocused, even bored, which was something he had never experienced. In the early afternoon, he fell asleep on the couch, holding a pile of papers. The sun deep was in the west when he woke, the papers strewn on the carpet beside him.

That night when sleep eluded him, he drove back to the diner. It was approaching 1 AM when he pulled into the parking lot and hid his car once more behind the parked trailer. Everything looked as it had the night before.

He sat and watched the comings and goings. The cars and trucks that stopped grew fewer, and by 2 almost no one was stopping. He watched the night waitress and the cook leave after their replacements arrived. He sat up every time he heard a vehicle on the highway. He waited till the sky in the east lightened, then he drove up to the diner, parked and went in for breakfast. The food was just as delicious as it had been the previous morning. He finished and sat back.

Why was he here? The food was excellent, sure, but why was he here now? He knew the 'why', but wasn't sure how to articulate it. It was the bikers. It was what he felt when he looked at them.

Years ago, he had been driving in the city. A biker dressed in leather and denim riding a chopper drove alongside him. He had a patch on his back. Simon did not remember what the patch looked like, nor what it said. He remembered how the biker was laying back his arms up high on the handlebars. There was a freedom that he, even then, knew he didn't have. He had watched the biker riding along until he turned off. The sight had never left him.

He smiled at the memory. The loud exhaust. The tall handlebars: apes, they were called. Apes. An old memory that he had mostly lost returned in small bits. He had been eight or nine, riding down his street on his banana bike with a sissy bar and ape hanger handlebars. Its seat was a rich red with gold metal flake. That bike had been his freedom. It was the first time in his life he had stopped counting and just flew. He flew down the road, pedalling as fast as he could. He loved that bike. Inside him, he felt a need to find those bikers and that freedom he had once had.

He paid and left, determined to return that night and every night till he found them.

Two things happened almost precisely at the same moment. The first was close by. A small girl was riding her tricycle and was struck by a rusty white car heading too fast down her tiny street. The driver jumped out of his car and found the little girl and her bike still under the car. He leaped back in the car and reversed several feet. He returned to the girl's body. She lay pushed up against the curb, almost full length. She didn't appear hurt, though her tricycle in the grass behind her was bent beyond recognition. The driver moved closer to the little girl. Her eyes flew around wildly until they fell on the driver's face. They stopped and looked into his eyes. A small smile touched her lips. A confused look crossed her face as a bubble formed on her lips, a brighter pink than any gum. When it popped, it splattered the driver with blood.

He jerked back, wiping his face. When he looked again, the little girl could not see him. He cried, kneeling in a pool of blood that spread from the tiny form.

The second happened miles away at the crossroads that was the cause of so much misery. It was broad daylight, an old man stood there cursing a man called The Judge, the man responsible for the crossroads. The old man's screamed curse was cut short by the heart attack. He fell forward onto his face. He lay on the cold blacktop until a half-ton driven by a wiry old farmer stopped. He loped up to the man prone on the pavement. After a minute, he bent forward and half-dragged, half-carried the ailing man to his truck.

The truck was not a fast truck, but the farmer pushed it as hard as he dared. By the time they stopped in front of the hospital, his vehicle was wheezing and smoking badly. The small hospital came alive when the farmer started yelling, banging on the hood as he ran around the front of his truck to the passenger door. White coated men and women ran out to help the farmer with the man slumped in his front seat. They pulled the man onto a stretcher.

At about the same time, Mr. White stood and looked at the little girl lying in the gutter. He wasn't a man of emotions or of sentimentality. He wasn't a man, but he was a being offended by waste. This was waste. He looked down the street where the driver had sped away. The smoke from his spinning tires still hung in the air.

Mr. White took the little girl's hand and led her to the river.

Minutes later, Mr. White walked unnoticed into the hospital. The man had succumbed to the heart attack and lay on a hospital bed covered in a white sheet. Standing beside Mr. White, looking at his own dead body, he turned, "Well, I guess I'm dead," He said to Mr. White.

"Come," Mr. White turned to go.

"I wanted to tell the Judge he was a son of a bitch," the man said, and he turned to follow Mr. White.

Mr. White paused, "Why is that?"

"He's a lying bastard! He took from me and never gave me what I asked for."

Mr. White smiled, "He is the Devil; that's his business."

"Is he? I talked wit my pa, and he said dat The Judge just sortah showed up a few years back, turning things ta shit round here." The man stood still, puffed up and defiant.

Mr. White had asked that very question many times. This area seemed to be unusually active for the Judge.

The man and Mr. White walked out of the hospital onto the black sands.

It was well past midnight. Simon sat in his POS in the shade of the trailer. He had parked in the same spot for several days. He was more tired than he had ever been. Now though, it wasn't insomnia but his search that kept him up at night. He wouldn't admit it, but he felt more focused than usual. He waited, watching the few vehicles come and go, yet, after an hour or so, there were no bikes.

Simon was starting to nod off. He jerked his head up, not sure how long he had been asleep. He glanced at his watch, yawned and reached for the ignition. It was time to go home.

He turned the car over when two bikes rode in, pulled up to the diner and went in. He didn't recognize them. They had crests on their backs, but he couldn't make them out from this distance.

He sat up and watched. Through the window of the diner, he watched the bikers sit in a booth. A few minutes later, four more bikers drove up. They had just stopped when another four bikes rumbled into the parking lot.

*Eight bikers plus two. Now there are ten.*

Simon sat and watched as the four men laughed and hugged and walked into the diner together. They greeted the two already seated and joined them. They all crowded around the single booth, some perched on the back of the seats.

An hour later, a lone bike slowed, its tailpipe snapping, and turned off the blacktop. Its small headlamp cut the dark as it rolled up to the diner and stopped. The bike roared and quieted. The man swung his leg over the bike and walked to the dinner.

Simon knew who this man was. This was Jacob. This was the man Simon wanted–no, needed–to speak to. Simon left his car and walked across the parking lot, watching the group of bikers as they greeted Jacob as he walked into the diner. Most stood greeting with smiles and arms raised.

The Mack cab-over truck careened into the parking lot and slammed into Simon. His head smacked against the grill of the big truck as the truck jammed onto its brakes. Simon was sent flying into the gas pumps. He smashed several feet off the ground, breaking glass and plastic with his body then he fell to the concrete. He did not get up.

The diner disgorged thirteen bikers. The trucker had jumped down from his cab to see what he had hit, turned to see a gang of bikers running toward him. He panicked, ran back to his truck and tried to climb in. He was pulled down by one of the bikers.

Jacob knelt beside Simon.

"He's alive. Brian, call 911."

Simon lay on the hard cement surrounded by shattered glass and splintered plastic. His eyes opened for a second, "Jacob? I need to ask you a question." He slipped into unconsciousness.

A day later, Mr. White walked up to a mangled, rusted white car. It was bent around a power pole. It had been travelling at an extreme speed when it failed to make the turn and slid sideways into the pole. Mr. White recognized the car. It was the same car that sped away from the small child.

The driver opened the door, stepped out, stumbled and looked back at his dead body still sitting in the mangled car. He stood confused. Mr. White walked up to him. The driver's pant knees were stiff with dried blood.

"Fuck! I'm dead?" The driver said. He looked at his body, then at Mr. White. "Who the fuck are you?"

Mr. White smiled, "I am Mr. White. I am…"

"Mr. White? Look fucker, who the fuck are you?" The driver turned, menacing Mr. White.

Mr. White touched him gently on the chest. The driver gasped, before crumpling to the ground.

"I'm sorry to tell you, you are no longer in charge. You are dead, which means I am in charge."

Mr. White looked at the driver as he stood.

"K sorry, ya OK. What happins now?"

"Well, now we leave." Mr. White turned and started walking.

The driver looked once more at his dead body, "This ain't right. That fucker is full of shit. I never got what he promised."

Mr. White stopped, "What's that?"

"The fucking Judge is full ah shit."

"Really? How so?" Mr. White turned and looked at the driver.

"He ain't the Real Judge, can't be. Iffin he were I'd ah gotten what I asked fer."

"And what was that?"

The man hesitated. He looked around, "I wanted ta kill people an not git caught. I wanted ta know what it were like."

"Well, you did not get caught." Mr. White turned away and continued walking.

"Ya but I weren't supposed ta die neither. Not no how, " he said." The driver shook his head, "He can't be da real deal, no sir." And he followed Mr. White across the black sands.

The man looked up when Simon's eye opened.

"It's good to see you are awake."

Simon didn't recognize the face looking down on him. Or did he? There was something familiar about the smile. It was an undeniably handsome face. Simon thought he looked like Jimi Hendrix. The man wasn't a doctor, dressed in a dark suit, not the ice cream green that doctors wore. Simon looked into those dark eyes and slipped back into unconsciousness.

When he woke again, he knew where he was and who was looking at him. This man was a doctor, short and slightly hunched. He had the air of a man who knew exactly who he was and what he was here to do. He looked at Simon with a neutral expression, "How are you feeling today?"

Simon found his throat was too dry to reply. The Doctor didn't seem too worried about an answer. He turned away and started talking with the nurse who was standing by.

"I'll come by later and see how you are coming along," he said as he gave Simon a light pat on the shoulder and left.

The nurse watched the Doctor leave, then brought Simon a glass of water, "Drink slowly."

Simon tried to reach for the glass and couldn't. His right arm was in a cast. He looked at the white plaster, surprised. The nurse extended the glass to his left hand. He took it. He drank a full glass, then nodded for another. The nurse hesitated, but she gave him another, "Ok, now lay back. You need rest. Doctor Krajden will come and see you a bit later, but now sleep."

Simon was tired. He slipped back into sleep easily and quickly.

It wasn't dark when he woke again. Outside his door, he could hear the sounds of the hospital continuing, though quieter. They felt hushed.

He looked at the ceiling. A light somewhere outside, maybe in the parking lot, cast long, thin shadows across the ceiling. Laying there, he tried to remember what had happened. He remembered seeing Jacob come to the diner. He remembered being excited that he was going to get to ask his question.

A noise to his right. He turned and saw a man sitting in the shadows.

"Good evening, Simon," the man stood, stepping into the small light, "How are you feeling?"

Simon recognized the man. This was the man that had been here before.

"I feel fine. Who are you?"

"You can call me Mr. White."

"Mr. White. Do I know you?" Simon tried to pull himself up and found he couldn't.

"Oh no, not yet. We won't meet professionally for some time." Mr. White smiled. He had a pleasant smile.

"In that case, may I ask…"

"What am I doing in your room? You see, I am called here quite frequently." He looked at Simon with a touch of sadness in his eyes, "I was here when you were brought in, actually."

"I can't quite remember what happened," Simon said. Looking down at his body hidden under the white and blue covers.

"You got hit by a truck. Quite a large truck, as I understand it. Threw you across a parking lot into some gas pumps. You were saved by a bunch of bikers."

"Bikers? Yes, I was hoping to talk to them." Simon looked up at Mr. White.

"Oh, why is that?" Mr. White leaned forward, interested.

"I wanted to ask Jacob a question." Simon tried again to sit up. Again, he failed. He glanced at Mr. White, puzzled, then reached down and touched his legs, he couldn't feel his touch. With a huge effort, he pushed himself to a sitting position and flung the covers aside. He patted his legs, reaching down to his knees. Simon looked at Mr. White. "Yes," he said slowly, "The truck severed your spine." then, as an afterthought, "sorry."
Mr. White opened his mouth to say more, but the door opened, and Doctor Krajden entered, followed by a nurse.

"I see you are awake."

"What happened? Why can I not feel my legs?" his voice was steady and calm.

"Well... You came in, in a very bad way. The attending Doctor wasn't sure you were going to make it. He rightfully diagnosed your injuries. You had severe fractures in your L1, L2, and L4 vertebrae, along with other fractures and multiple contusions. The fractures in your spine caused a complete disruption of the spinal cord, which has led to a state of paraplegia."

Simon looked at him, his brow furrowed.

"Unfortunately, you will be confined to a wheelchair for the rest of your life," the Doctor said.

Simon looked at him. He wasn't shocked or even really upset. Doctor Krajden continued talking, hardly looking at Simon. He looked at the nurse, who had a sad, sympathetic look on her face. He looked for Mr. White. Mr. White was gone.

A few days later, Simon was reading when there was some sort of commotion in the hallway right outside his door. The door burst open, and the room filled with leather-clad bikers, led by Jacob. Behind Jacob was the largest man Simon had ever seen. He was at least a head taller than Jacob, who was well over six foot.

"Me ann da boys cum ta see how yer doin'," Jacob said. "Doc says yer gonna be riding yer own set ah wheels from now on."

"Were gonna havfta trick 'em out fer ya," said the mountain of a man. He was grinning from ear to ear, though the grin seemed forced. There was pain in those eyes.

"Ah ya, this here is Brian," Jacob said.

The Jurors hung around for 32 minutes, laughing and joking. They had brought him a bunch of weird, slightly offensive gifts, but one thing they brought was a denim vest with the Juror's crest on the back.

"This ain't sumpin we do often, well, in fact, we never dun it but this here is yer kut. Wer makin you an honorary member of the Jurors," Jacob held out the vest with a certain reverence. Simon took it with his good arm and looked at it spread out on his lap. He was touched. It was such a simple thing; however, he felt like he belonged for the first time.

As if they were embarrassed by what they had done, they said their goodbye and noisily filed out. Simon looked at the vest, enjoying the feel. He looked up and was surprised to see Brian standing awkwardly by the door.

Simon looked at him. It was apparent he had something to say. Simon waited.

"Hum… I know this sucks. I know how you feel," Brian paused, "Umm… yer from 'round, right?"

"Yes," Simon said, not sure where he was going. Two hums.

"Umm… ah mean you knowd about the Judge."

"Yes," Simon perked up a bit. Three hums.

"Look, Jacob don't want me talking to ya, none of the Jurors do. They're all got their reasons to have a powerful hate-on fer The Judge but dey know what appened an know how I feel. Dey ain't gonna stop me," Brian smiled a bit, sheepishly. It was the most words he had spoken all in one time. Simon did not know what to say.

"Back a few years ago, I lost ma arms. Got em torn off in ah bailer." Brian stepped forward as if to show he still had his arms.

"I went to the Judge," he said, "Ah mean, the only ting I could do was live wit it an put my Ma through hell or swallow a lead pill."

Simon waited. Brian looked down at his arms. They were massive, like the rest of him.

"I want to go to see the Judge," Simon said.

"Ya I thought you might," Brian looked down at the floor, then back up to Simon. "Ah gatta tell ya what appened next. Ya, see, not only did I sell ma soul, but days after my Ma an Pa were kilt. There's a sorta balance. You get one thin', and somethin else bad happns."

Brian watched Simon for a minute.

"It's not what you think, but I still want to see him," Simon said.

"Sure, sure, k. When you got out, I'll drive ya over. But think on it. There's no goin' back," Brian smiled, head down, turned and walked out of the room.

Simon was trying to sleep. He stared, watching the light shift on the ceiling. He had spent the last several nights unable to sleep, unable to do anything about it. The nurse had offered him pills to help. He had refused. He had tried drugs some years back and had hated the way he felt the next day. He swore never again.

He heard a noise in his room and turned to see Mr. White standing in the room, just barely visible in the shadows.

"So, you have made a decision," Mr. White said.

"Mr. White."

"Feeling better?" Mr. White said.

"I'm fine," Simon said, "What do you mean 'a decision'?"

"You are going to see the Judge, but not for the reason everyone thinks."

Simon frowned, "Humm? I... What do you mean?"

"Oh Simon, I know many things. I have certain connections, you see," Mr. White smiled.

"Who are you, Mr. White?"

"Simon, Simon, you know who I am, what I am."

Simon realized he did. He knew who this was. "You are Death," he said.

"Very good. Now let's talk. I have a proposal for you."

Simon sat at the crossroads. His chair gleamed in the dark. Brian had picked him up at the hospital the morning he was released. They had driven to a tavern called the Ol' Scratch on 11. Simon had driven by it many times but never stopped.

Brian pushed Simon into the bar wearing his kut. Several of the Jurors were there waiting for him. They cheered to see him. Simon could not remember being this happy. He felt he was part of something, something great and wonderful. They sat around drinking coffee, then switched to beer late in the afternoon.

Jacob walked in just as food arrived. He smiled, slapped Simon on the back and sat. The Jurors gathered as if they had been waiting for Jacob to arrive.

"So I know yer minds made up an all. An we would be the last sorry bunch to be try to talk ya outta what yer set ta do," he paused and looked around the group, "but I think you should no a few thins."

And he told Simon his story, told about why he had sold his soul and what had happened. Each Juror took his turn. Each told his story, each talked about their regret. Each told how they would turn back the clock and stop themselves from going to the crossroads. Simon listened to each story. He listened to each regret.

*Thirteen stories. Thirteen regrets.*

They were quiet for a minute, then Jacob said, "Ok, ah think we need another round. An I need another order of hot wings."

The night raced by. Simon laughed and forgot to count, even forgot to make a list or even think about lists. When

184

Brian's face went serious, he stood up. The Jurors went silent. Around them, the bar continued, but it was muffled. The bar's buzz seemed distant, quieted.

"Let's git goin'," Brian said. Jacob stood beside Simon. "See you in a bit, Simon," Jacob said.

Simon sat at the crossroads, waiting for a being that would change his life. He was excited, anticipating the meeting ahead. It happened between blinks. One second he was sitting in the dark; the next he was engulfed in noise and light. He raised his left arm in defence and closed his eyes. The noise died, and the lights blinked off. He lowered his arm, opened his eyes and realized a car was inches from his knees.

The grill had a yellow bow tie shape right in the middle at almost eye level to him. He felt the heat of the engine and could smell the hot metal.

Simon rolled back from the car as a man climbed out.

"Well, howdy, Simon. I heard you were coming to see me." The man was tall, slim and handsome, sheathed in a black suit. His white shirt glowed in the night air. "I am sorry for your troubles," he said, "and yes, I can get you what you want." Simon looked up at him, "You are the Judge?"

"I am."

"You are not what I expected," Simon said.

"Did you expect horns and a tail?"

"No, but not you."

"Well, I am the Judge. What can I do you for?" He

stepped forward and smiled, his teeth as white as his shirt, "I'm guessing you want your legs back."

Simon looked at the Judge for a minute. "No," he said, "that's not what I want from you."

"Oh!" Surprise showed on the Judge's face. He recovered. "Then what is it you want?"

Simon smiled, "I want a list."

"A list?"

"Yes, a list that no one has or ever will have."

"Ok, that is a first, I must say." The Judge straightened his already straight tie.

"I want a list of every soul you have collected from these parts."

The Judge looked at Simon for a minute, "That's right, you have a thing about lists and numbers." He smiled.

Beside and slightly behind him, a man formed. It looked as though hundreds of black shapes swirled around, gathering into the body of a man. Simon heard a buzzing sound and realized the shapes were black flies. They formed the man as tall as the Judge, slimmer, dressed in a suit and a large-brimmed hat. He was holding a book. He was smiling.

"Sir, I am Mr. July. Do we have a contract?" The man said as the buzzing faded.

"Mr. July, yes. Give Simon here your book,"

"Sir?" Mr. July's smiled faltered, his head turned toward the Judge, "My book?"

"Yes. YOUR book." Anger flared briefly in the Judge's eyes. His smile slipped for a second, then returned.

"Yes sir." He stepped forward and extended his black book towards Simon. Simon took it. The book writhed in his hand, several flies crawled up his hand. Simon could feel his fingers slightly sink into the book.

"Is this going to vanish when you leave?" Simon asked. The Judge frowned, then reached forward and touched the book. It immediately solidified into a black leather-bound book.

Mr. July stood holding his book. Simon looked at it then looked down in his hands at the leather book he held. They looked the same. Mr. July smiled.

"I believe you had a second request?" The Judge said, his smile back in all its ghastly glory.

"Yes. I have played the lottery for years now. I want to win."

"HA! Of course. That's a simple one. What number do you play?"

"790879."

"A prime. Very nice," the Judge reached into his jacket and pulled out a slip of paper. He handed it to Simon. "Here you go."

The three men looked at each other for a minute, then the Judge turned and climbed into his car. Mr. July slumped, then fell forward. He never hit the ground. He broke up into a cloud of flies.

When Simon looked away from the cloud of flies, the Judge and his shiny black car were pulling away down the highway.

Simon sat staring at the surrounding night. He was pleased. He held his book, his list in his hand, along with the winning lottery ticket. It's all he really ever wanted.

In the distance, he could see headlights coming towards him. That would be Brian coming to pick him up. After a minute, Simon could hear the big truck's exhaust.

Brian shifted down, and the truck's rumble rose in pitch. The truck lurched, then a squeal of tires and a yelp. The pickup came to a stop. Simon watched as Brian climbed out and stepped into the headlights. Even at this distance, Simon heard Brian's curse.

After a second, Brian shook his head, turned and climbed back in, reversed, then drove around something on the road. He pulled up close to Simon.

When Brian climbed out of his truck and walked towards Simon, there was surprise on his face.

"Yer still in yer chair," he said.

Simon looked down at the chair. He looked up at Brian, "Yes. That's not why I came here. I came for this." He held up his book, a broad smile on his face.

"Ah don't git it," Brian said.

"No, I don't suppose you would, Brian," Mr. White walked past Brian's truck and stood beside Simon.

"Mr. White! Ah, that's why the rabbit." Brian looked back down the road at the small shape he had driven around.

"Yes," Mr. White said, "I need to be called by a dying."

"But a bunny rabbit?" Brian whined.

"Sorry." Mr. White looked momentarily uncomfortable. "It was the closest creature around when you came."

"Brian," Simon said, "Brian. You have been so nice to me. Your friendship, however brief, was absolutely wonderful. I have never felt accepted like I have since you and the Jurors came into my life." A tear burned in Simon's eye. "You will never know how much being with you and the boys meant to me, but I have made a deal. One that I didn't think you would understand."

"How kin ya say dat. We all had made a deal with that fucker!" Brian's voice rose.

"No, Brian, not with the Judge. With Mr. White, with Death."

"Ah don't git it," Brian frowned.

"When I was in the parking lot before, that truck. That's what I wanted. I was going to come into the diner and ask for your help to find the Judge. Then the truck happened, and things shifted a bit. Mr. White and I spoke at the hospital. He offered me a deal I couldn't say no to." Simon smiled up at Mr. White. He looked at Brian and smiled, "Here. I hope this is in a small way 'thanks' for all you and the Jurors have done for me." Simon extended his hand.

Brian stepped forward and took the lottery ticket. He looked at Simon, puzzled.

"It's a winning ticket that should give you guys enough to maybe build a meeting house or a garage or whatever," Simon smiled, "and now it's time I go, I guess," He looked up at Mr. White.

"Yes."

Simon stood, book in hand, no cast on his arm, and looked back at his slumped body in his wheelchair.

"Brian, would you deal with that for me," Simon said, indicating his dead body, "I have no further use for it. You see, I am now Death's accountant. I will count the dead."

Simon smiled at Brian, waved and walked into blackness with Mr. White.

# A LEAD PILL

So tallwalker. Yer done Yessir Yesir,
dats it
Hopin' you lik'd it ver good.
Peck 'er to leave a rear view
Ver fine

Photo by Sheri Belanger

## About the Author

After leaving the Northern forest and farmland of Saskatchewan, Rick headed to Calgary and the Alberta College of Art. After 4 years of hard work, he came out confused and somewhat lost. Now what?

Rick has been a bouncer (one week), he has been a radio switcher (one night), and worked at the CBC (one month). He was a stuntman (2 action movies that he never saw, but he's not alone in that) and he modelled briefly (he was the Jolly Green Giant for a time). Rick has built houses, packed groceries, cut grass and has written four, and illustrated 19 children's books. He has worked as a painter, a designer, an illustrator and a writer.

Rick has won awards for his work in advertising and publishing, including the Ruth Schwartz Award, the Amelia Frances Howard-Gibbon Award and numerous national and international awards including the Toronto Art Directors' Awards, Communication Arts Magazine's Award of Excellence, American Illustration Award of Excellence, and the New York Art Directors' Award of Excellence. He has been featured in Smithsonian Magazine, Applied Arts Magazine and in The Artist's Magazine. His commissioned portraits include Robertson Davies, Margaret Atwood, Christopher Ondaatje, and David Thomson.

Rick is currently working on his novel 'HARD PLACE' and a graphic novel of the same title, to be released at the end of October, 2021.

For 'Hard Place' updates, sign up at deadcatstud.io.

## Acknowledgments

Without my friends and family reading and correcting it, this collection would never have happened.

Sunny once again poured over each of the stories, correcting, suggesting and just supporting.

Noah stepped up and added his prodigious wordsmithing abilities, and also laid down some perfectly spectacular guitar tracks to accompany the audio version.

Justin was untiring when I needed an editor. He spent much of his off-time lost in this world, finding the confusing or just wrong words.

Ken Cade became my guy for the podcast. He took it off my shoulders and made it come to life.

Jeff gave me access to his vast knowledge of sound and editing.

Maite coached me brilliantly as I struggled to find a voice to give the characters I had released onto the page.

Mercedes became my first beta reader and forged through what must have been a trial of fire.

Mike helped with my underwhelming marketing, and made it actually work.


Thank you for all the love and support.
Sunniva Foley
Justin Ramsden
Noah Zacharin
Ken Cade
Jeff Bessner
Mike Jacobson
Maite Jacobson
Mercedes Jacobson
Mike Jacobson
Laura Fernandez

# Other books by R A Jacobson

'A Single Round'
is available as digital, softcover, hardcover and
audiobook.

Click here

'A Single Round'
the audiobook
will be released January, 2021 and will be available
where ever you get your audiobooks.
Sign up to be notified.

Click here

'A Lead Pill'
will be released march 25 th, 2021 and will be available
for free for a limited time.
Sign up to be notified.

Click here

'HARD PLACE'
will be released October, 2021 and will be available
for free for a limited time.
Sign up to be notified.

Click here